ISBN-13:978-0-578-74147-5
ISBN-10:0578741474

Cover design by: Rayne Beaux Art
Library of Congress Control Number: 2018675309
Printed in the United States of America

This book is dedicated to all the Christians who have the vision and compassion to go Beyond the walls of the church and serve those around them, especially in their own communities. It is specifically dedicated to Jim and Rebekah Matuga, who had the vision and dedication to lead Chestnut Ridge Church Beyond its walls to those in need in Morgantown and West Virginia.

It is also dedicated to Tonya Wolfe. When I ran out of ideas to write about for this book, she was a ready source of situations I was not aware of occurring within a few miles of where I live. She also suggested including a list of resources of how to become involved with different outreaches for these issues to make it easier to make a difference in someone's life, and willingly spent hours looking up information on these groups while I continued writing.

The last person this book is dedicated to is Ruth Bucklew, who spent hours editing the the book and whose suggestions made the rewriting process easier and more focused.

CONTENTS

FOREWORD

Many modern Christians view the church as a place to get help, essentially an emotional hospital. They go where the music makes them feel happy, the preaching massages their self image, at least a few people consistently say nice things to them, and there is little demand for time or money commitments. While these things are helpful in staying focused in life, making them your focus turns the church from learning about how to grow your relationship with Jesus Christ into a religion of self-actualization.

Church should be a place for people to heal. The healing should not be based on feeling better about what they have done, but allowing Holy Spirit to change the attitudes and beliefs that caused them to mess up in the first place as we submit to God's leading in their lives. The purpose of meeting together should focus on learning from God's word instead of temporarily easing our consciences.

The church should not just be a hospital, however. It was designed to be a training center where Christians are educated about how to reach out to others with similar problems outside the walls and schedule of its services. It would be better if we view it as a teaching hospital, where we develop the skills and knowledge to help others-and have access to take care of our own issues as needed.

Too often the focus of churches is on helping people in far away places. Local issues are simply presented as prayer requests, requests that are frequently forgotten before we leave the service. The big ugly issues are simply overlooked, and if they affect someone inside the church they are either not talked about or brushed over in euphemisms as we insist to those affected they will resolve themselves if they pray hard enough.

That is not how Jesus handled the problems he encountered, however. He sought out people in the middle of their problems and dealt directly with them, whether it was illness, evil spirits, social woes or even death. The purpose of this book is to challenge Christians who enjoy their social and religious comfort zones to follow the example of Christ by digging out the ugly realities of life in our own communities and asking God to lead them in the ways most effective in changing those realities.

As I suggested in my previous book "The Financial Cornerstone," it is better to focus your giving on issues you are personally concerned about instead of spreading your contributions over many different issues. It is also more effective to support local efforts with your giving and time than it is to contribute to national groups with larger overheads and few incentives to help those in your area. This is not an attempt to get everyone to contribute to all the resources discussed in this book, but to chose one or two local groups who work with causes that make your heart burn and contribute to them with your time, money and influence.

1. THE TRASH BAG KID

Leroy Thomas got off the school bus in front of his Market Place Court apartment. He climbed the steps to the second floor, walking around bits of trash laying by a few of the apartment doors in the light brown buildings. Occasional holes pitted the walls, and the stains of spilled drinks and cigarette burns hinted at the years of delayed maintenance and neglect it had suffered. Music beat through the walls of the apartment next to theirs, muffling both the sounds of fighting from the apartment below and the disjointed mutterings of the rarely-seen occupant inside.

He slipped the key out of his pocket when he reached his apartment, wondering what he would find inside today. "Hi Mom," he called. The walls just stared back at him in silence. Even though he did not know where his parents were, he knew why they had left. The stifling heat and large "Keep Out" sign on what used to be his bedroom told him they had cooked a batch of meth and gone out to escape the fumes, hoping to sell enough to buy what they needed to make the next one.

He sighed as he laid his math book on the kitchen counter. He opened the fridge and cupboards looking for something to snack on, but all the money had been spent on making meth. Homework would have to wait. He would probably be on his own all night, so he needed to get some food to eat before it became dark and too dangerous to be outside.

Leroy picked up a garbage bag from the floor of the apartment on his way out. He began kicking through the scattered trash in the hallway, putting the aluminum cans he found into the bag after crushing them. It looked like someone had already gone through his building, so he went through other buildings in the complex. When he found enough to fill his bag, he walked a few blocks down Mack Avenue to City Recycling to trade them in for cash. He didn't get much, but the price of aluminum was up today so it was more than usual.

Leroy stuffed the money deep into his pocket, then headed back down the avenue. He turned left on Rivard Street, the walked two blocks to Frank's Meat and Produce. He took his time going down the aisle, finally settling on two packages of tuna and a loaf of bread. There was just enough left to buy an ice cream sandwich, a rare treat for the warm fall afternoon. After paying for the food he walked back to his apartment, but the ice cream sandwich didn't survive the trip.

Once he was back in the apartment, Leroy tore open the fish and spread it on four pieces of bread. A little mayonnaise would have been helpful, but the flavoring in the tuna helped it go down. When he finished eating, he washed the knife and put the rest of the bread on top of the refrigerator to hide it from the cockroaches which occasionally invaded the kitchen. One good thing about his parents making meth was the fumes tended to kill the bugs nearby.

Leroy cleaned off the table and opened his math book. As he struggled through his last set of problems there was a sharp knock on the door. A knock like that usually meant trouble, so he went to his parent's room to hide instead of answering it.

Hiding did not help this time, however. It was the police with a search warrant, and they were on a mission. After knocking several times and demanding the door be opened, the flimsy door frame shattered with a single kick from a practiced officer. Within seconds the officers had gone through the five rooms of the apartment, and Leroy had been dragged out of his parent's closet to a kitchen table chair.

When the police opened the door to his bedroom, they found his bed leaning against the wall and his desk covered with hot plates and glassware. Empty liter pop bottles lay on the floor amongst bottles and cans of meth ingredients, and a dented can of Coleman fuel dripped onto the stained carpet.

Empty cold medicine boxes cascaded up one corner, probable evidence of the pharmacy robbery that had happened two days ago. After confirming nobody was hiding in it, the police backed out and secured the room.

Before the HazMat team arrived, the police told Leroy to get a trash bag and put everything he needed in it. The math and other homework from the table went in first. There was a pile of unfolded laundry on the couch he was able to pull a couple shirts and shorts from, along with some underwear. The bathroom had chemicals in it, so his toothbrush and shampoo was too contaminated to take. So was all of the toys and clothes in his bedroom. With his relatively clean belongings now inside the black plastic prison, everyone evacuated the apartment.

When they were seated safely outside on a bench by the street, the police confirmed his parents were in jail for selling meth. With the contents of the apartment added in, they would be there for several years. He was now officially one of the faceless members of the Detroit foster care system, unless one of his relatives stepped forward to take care of him.

The HazMat team came and began collecting evidence in the apartment. An officer took Leroy's trash bag out to the police car and put it in the trunk. Leroy got in the back seat and headed down to the Third Precinct station. He would be there a while, answering questions about what he knew about his parent's drug making and dealing. He had stayed away from it as much as he could, so it shouldn't take long.

When all the questions had been answered for the fourth or fifth time, they stopped. A member of the Paul Martin Home came into the station, looking for the most recent victim of the drug war. They took Leroy and his trash bag to the home where the staff was hard at work trying to squeeze him into a temporary spot until a more permanent home could be found. The list of kids coming into the system had been growing faster than those leaving so it was a struggle.

When they arrived at the home, he took his garbage bag into the conference room and pulled his history book out to finish his homework. No matter where he spent the night, the next day he would be back in the classroom and he was one of the few kids the teacher expected to turn their work in. One thing his Mom always told him was to do his homework and succeed in school so he could escape from the neighborhood and have a good life.

One of the staff brought a suitcase in and told Leroy to put his stuff in it. Someone had donated it to the home for this kind of situation. When he opened it, he got another surprise. Inside was a toothbrush, some toothpaste and soap, and new clothes with the tags still on them. There was even a football and some other toys in it as well, so he had things to play with. In the corner was a Bible with the plastic still on it. Someone's generosity helped ease the pain from losing his own stuff, but it was still hard not knowing when he would see his parents again.

There was a group of men doing some maintenance in the home as Leroy waited to be picked up by his foster parents. He could hear them talking down the hallway, joking about the Lions and who they needed to trade for to do well this season. Leroy liked sports more than reading about wars so the typing on his school computer slowed to a crawl as he listened to the banter.

The leader saw Leroy watching them and walked over to him. "Hi, I'm Jesus," he said. "What are you in for?"

"My parents got busted for drugs today," Leroy answered. "Now I'm doing homework until someone takes me to their home."

"Doesn't look like you are doing much homework now," Jesus observed. "What are you studying?"

"Oh, the Crusades," Leroy answered. "Seems kind of silly and sad to go to war over something like that."

"You are right," Jesus said. "They had it all wrong. They went to war mostly because there more men than there were jobs for them to fill."

"Oh, that makes more sense," Leroy responded. "I guess it was a good way to get rid of a bunch of them."

"The couple that are going to take you home tonight are almost here," Jesus said. "I want you to promise me this. Say your prayers every night, do what you know is right, and follow the rules of the house where you are. Can you do that for me?"

"Yes," Leroy nodded. "But it will be hard. I miss my parents, even though I know what they did was wrong."

"You will, and you should." Jesus said. "You will see them again in the future, but they can't take care of you right now. Just remember I will always be there for you, so just think of me when you are having a rough time."

"Ok, I will," Leroy answered. "But I don't even know who you are."

"That's ok, you will find out soon," Jesus replied. "I have to go back to painting now, and it's time for you to go." As he turned to leave, he put one hand on Leroy's shoulder and the other on his new suitcase. "Even though you lost most of your things, you have everything you need for now."

As Jesus took his first step back down the hallway, the doorbell rang. The lady in charge opened it, and it was Leroy's foster parents. She brought them in and introduced them, then took them aside to let them know what had happened with him.

As they were talking Leroy closed his homework and started to put it in his suitcase. The contents seemed different somehow. He looked inside, and the clothes were the style he liked. There was a new pair of tennis shoes he didn't remember seeing before as well. He put his books and computer into the bag and zipped it closed, ready for the last leg of his journey for the day.

The lady in charge rushed Leroy and his temporary family out the door, eager to get away from the stresses of her job for the day. As they walked down the hallway Jesus smiled at him, and Leroy said, "Thank you," and gave him a big thumbs up. Then he followed the couple out the door, wondering what this part of his new life would be like.

Reflections

Titus 3:3 At one time we too were foolish, disobedient, deceived and enslaved by all kinds of passions and pleasures. We lived in malice and envy, being hated and hating one another.

As the numbers grow for drug overdoses and drug-related suicides, it is easy to forget about the hidden casualties behind the numbers. Taylor County, West Virginia has a relatively small population density with around seventeen thousand people in it. In 2019 there were over six hundred children in homes with known drug users. Some of them have been placed in foster care due to their parents dying of overdoses, unsafe living conditions and neglect.

Children can be removed from homes for non-drug related reasons as well. These can include abuse and their parents being arrested for other crimes. No matter the cause, there are many situations where they are taken with either minimal belongings or even just the clothes on their backs. The large number of kids in the foster system makes it difficult for the state to provide all of the resources kids need when they are relocated.

Questions for Contemplation

1. Have you heard the term "trash bag kids" before? What kind of things or images does this bring to your mind?

2. Even in areas without high drug abuse, the number of children in foster care are significant. There tend

to be more in urban areas, but that is not always the case. What resources are available in your community to help families who care for foster kids?

3. Agencies responsible for monitoring children in high-risk circumstances are notoriously over-worked and kids can fall through the cracks. What are some ways we can ensure kids who need help get the resources they need?

4. After school programs play an important role in providing healthy role models and meaningful ac-tivities, such as the sports programs mentioned earlier in the book. What programs are available for kids in your community?

5. Religious values are frequently missing in the lives of high-risk children. Many foster homes have strong religious foundations, but it is difficult to instill religious values in children when they are only there temporarily. What ways can the church community help foster parents positively influence children when they are temporarily placed in a home of one of their attendees?

Call to Action

The best and most important step you can take to assist children in the foster care system is to keep as many out of it as possible. The first way to help is to ensure children in your home, and those you interact with, grow up in a safe environment free from drug abuse and other harmful situations. If you have an issue you are dealing with, such as drug use, follow the first rule of parenting and get help dealing with it before it creates any more problems in your own home.

Providing resources for kids who are removed from homes is also important. You can buy suitcases and fill them with hygiene items, clothes and toys for those forced to leave in a hurry. Most school districts have backpack programs where backpacks full of food, hygiene items and clothes are given out to kids in need on weekends or over vacations, and foster kids usually qualify to receive them. Volunteering in your children's programs at church or as mentors or tutors are other ways to help provide positive environments for not only foster kids, but all of the kids in your community.

There are several organizations and ministries who focus on foster kids. Perhaps the most common of them is Court-Appointed Special Advocates (CASA), who have long-term relationships with one or more children and help them go through the legal process. Together We Rise is a ministry focused on caring for foster children. If you are unable to find a local ministry for foster children, contact your local Department of Health and Human Resources (DHHR) or Child Protective Services (CPS) agency to find out what needs they have that you can help fill.

2. THE CRACK HOUSE

The chill of late fall penetrated their exposed skin as thirteen men trudged down Main Street in Grafton. Fog rising from the Tygart River wrapped tendrils of depression over the town, accented by the boarded-up windows of abandoned businesses covered by grunge from the coal cars trickling through the switching yard of what was once a booming railroad town.

Judas nudged Jesus as they passed Leonard's Grill, sparsely furnished with a stainless-steel counter and wooden picnic tables. Jesus shook his head and walked on, picking up the pace a bit to fight the intensifying cold. There was a more urgent nudge as they passed Espresso Yourself, the lone coffee shop in town, as they flipped the "Closed" sign. There was an audible collective groan as they strolled past the Capri Pizza Parlor with its smudged windows and stained walls. Jesus said, "Not yet" and kept walking.

They continued up the hill at the end of the short business district, curving past the old fire station halfway up. They took a sharp right onto Mulligan Street, passing a mix of houses ranging from modern and neatly kept to abandoned with windows boarded up and rusting cars in their yards. There were still three times more abandoned houses than churches in town, even though it was decades after the railroad boom ended.

Jesus started pointing out houses as he walked by. "One in that house," he said. "Two over there, with three young kids," as he passed a grungy red house. "Three were there until they OD'd last month," pointing at a blue house with weeds starting to close in on it. "She would have become an orphan last night if it hadn't been for NarCan," he said, pointing at a three-year-old girl sitting on a porch around the corner.

"Here we are," he announced, heading up a sidewalk surrounded by waist-high weeds leading to a house with plywood falling off the broken windows. The front door sagged on a broken top hinge, scraping an arc on the sagging wooden floor beneath it. Smoke from candles and a fire in the crumbling fireplace flooded the living room, stirred into chaos as three people ran out of the room at the sight of strangers.

The room was not empty, however. A girl in her twenties lay half-covered by a blanket in the corner, moaning in pain. A gray-haired man curled up under the broken window, eyes glazed as he gasped for air. Without glancing at either of them, Jesus walked through the room to a set of rickety stairs leading to the second floor. John and Peter followed him, while the others tried to find a spot without broken glass or discarded needles to wait.

The second floor was colder and darker than the first, with years of dust disturbed by trails of footprints to the rooms still somewhat habitable. Jesus walked to the end of the hall, glancing at the people passed out in the other rooms as he walked by.

There was a man in his thirties in the end room with a tourniquet on his arm holding a syringe full of heroin. His head was thrown back, dirty blond hair dripping with sweat and his face contorted in agony. His stomach muscles twitched in withdrawal, feeling like they were on fire. He held the needle to his arm but pled with God to give him an escape from his torment.

"Peace, my son," Jesus said as he entered the room. He walked over to the man and took the syringe and tourniquet from him. As he touched him, the muscle spasms ended, and the look of agony left his face. Sobbing, he collapsed onto Jesus and held him in a tight embrace. As he wept on Jesus's shoulder the pock marks on his face faded and the sunken eyes of addiction filled in. When he released his hug moments later a healthy man stood there, the fire of life once again burning in his eyes.

"Let's go get some pizza," Jesus said. "Finally," Peter muttered under his breath. They left the room, intent on their de-

sire for food. As they walked by each room Jesus glanced into it, shook his head and walked on. As they exited the stairs Jesus looked at the man gasping for air by the window and simply said, "The fifth one in this house so far."

Rejoined by the rest of the group, Jesus and the man healed from addiction walked towards the pizza shop. The man began telling them his life story along the way. As they turned the corner onto Main Street an ambulance and police car maneuvered around the corner with lights and sirens blazing, heading towards the crack house they just left.

When they reached Capri's, they pushed a couple tables together in the near-empty room. Judas went to the counter and ordered the cheapest pizzas available, with water to drink. The man continued his story, weaving a tale of depression and desperation. As he talked the staff of the restaurant kept looking at him, conversing in the back.

When their pizzas were ready, the waitress and owner approached the table with their food. They asked the man if he was John, and he said yes. They knew him well but were amazed at his transformation. They said he looked like he used to five years ago, before he had gotten into drugs. The owner offered him a job, so he lost his addiction and unemployment on the same day.

As the food disappeared from the platters, John finished his life story and asked the group about their adventures. When all stomachs were full and the conversation waned, John asked the question that had been running through his mind. "Tell me," he said, "Why did you pick me? There were at least ten other addicts in that house, so why did you only save me?"

Jesus gave him a simple answer. "Everyone had the same problem. You were all addicted to heroin. They only reason I came to your room and didn't help the others was, everyone else was seeking salvation in their next fix. You were the only person asking God for the real solution to your problem. That is why you were saved, but I couldn't help the others."

As closing time approached, the group got up and left.

John headed to the house where his wife and kids waited, wondering if today would be the last day they saw him alive. Jesus and the disciples turned right and headed the mile up the hill to Crislip Motor Lodge, the only place to stay in town. The cold was more intense now as the fog thickened but knowing another life had been saved kept them warm as they covered the distance to where they were staying.

Reflections

Proverbs 21:17 Whoever loves pleasure will become poor; whoever loves wine and olive oil will never be rich.

Drug overdose has been one of the leading causes of death in the United States for several years. There are many factors which have contributed to this trend, including depressed economic conditions, high unemployment, high rates of opioid prescriptions for many years and more potent drugs. As of now employment rates have increased, the economy has improved in many areas and strict guidelines imposed for prescribing opioids. Despite improving cultural conditions, the rate of overdoses and related suicides continues to rise.

Drug abuse is driven by addiction. Technically alcohol is also a drug, but different programs have been developed to help people deal with the problem. While these programs are helpful and have helped thousands stop using drugs, many only address the spiritual aspect from a "higher power" aspect. Drug use opens the door to demon possession, which explains the superhuman strength and immunity to pain seen in advanced addiction. This is why treatment with a Christian basis is important to overcome this problem.

Part of the problem with churches reaching out to drug addicts is they don't understand the physical aspects of addiction. Cigarette smokers become addicted because nicotine stimulates brain centers that make them feel good. With many opioids and painkillers the effect is much more potent, because the drug essentially sets off all the reward centers of your meso-limbic system at once. This causes them to experience the highest level of euphoria. The problem with this type of addiction is, the effects of the drug fades with each hit so they have to take higher doses each time to get the same high. Overdoses frequently happen when someone's body cannot handle the other physical effects of the drug. Even if addicts stop taking drugs, the inability to feel the same intense pleasure frequently causes them to commit suicide.

Questions for Contemplation

1. What are the drug addiction treatment programs available in your area? How many of them are affiliated with churches or other Christian ministries?

2. How does knowing that addiction is linked to demonic possession affect your thinking about addiction and how it should be treated?

3. Does knowing how opioids and similar drugs affects the mind change your understanding of why it is so difficult for addicts to quit using them? In what ways?

4. Considering the physical effects of taking drugs on the mind and how it drives suicide rates of those who become clean, what roles can the church take to address

the feeling of emptiness that comes from being sober?

5. Prayer is the fallback prescription for any woe, and there are good reasons for it. How does understanding the addiction process better help you realize the need for addicts to have ongoing assistance from professionally trained counselors to address their needs?

Call to Action

There are many Christian programs available to help treat addicts. One of my cousins developed Brian's Safehouse and The Sparrow's Nest in Mount Hope, West Virginia after losing their son to addiction. Olive Branch Mission in Chicago, Illinois has local and international outreach programs. Mercy Multiplied is a program based in Nashville, Tennessee for women with outreach programs nationwide. The Dream Center is based in Los Angeles, California and has affiliated programs nationwide. Perhaps the program with the most local treatment centers is Teen Challenge, which accepts all ages for their program.

It is expensive for churches and ministries to maintain addiction treatment programs to help people stop being dependent on drugs. Follow up programs are heavily dependent on volunteers to provide ongoing support once graduates re-enter normal life. There is always a need for ongoing financial support to keep the programs functioning, and volunteers to maintain facilities and resources.

There is also a need for businesses to hire former addicts so they can support themselves and regain their self-worth. This is a significant part of their recovery process which can be complicated if they develop a criminal history of theft or violence while they are on drugs.

The church is called to accept people who become Christians and not hold their former lifestyles against them. This is as relevant for drug addicts as it is for someone who steals a car or commits adultery. Treating everyone as equals under God's eyes also is an important part of the recovery process that each one of us are responsible to do.

3. PEANUT PARK

It was a typical summer day in Chicago. The eighty-six-degree heat was exceeded by the humidity, creating an unpleasant haze that stifled anyone brave enough to leave the air-conditioned concrete jungle. Even the light breeze blowing off Lake Michigan just fluttered the curtains of mist without bringing any relief. Between the heavy humidity and intense sunlight reflecting off the water, traffic outside the skyscrapers crawled in an overheated sulk.

Not everyone could hide behind air conditioning, though. A group of thirteen headed towards Peanut Park after spending the night at the Pacific Garden Mission. They were in line early enough the night before to get free meals and beds in return for sitting through the church service with other homeless men. Now they took a bus down Canal Street until they got to Monroe Street. They chose to walk the rest of the way to the park, stopping to eat lunch at a McDonalds on the way. The break from the heat cooled them down enough to stop sweating, but the heat radiating off the sidewalk and buildings brought the unpleasantness back almost as soon as they stepped back into the sunshine.

Signs of the homeless were scattered along their way. A large cardboard box sagged against the side exit of a run-down apartment building, wilting under the dual attack of incessant sunshine and humidity. A crumpled pile of newspapers was stuffed behind the drainpipe of an office building. The base of the Office Depot loading dock was lined with empty bags of chips and other junk food. The shadow of an arched walkway between two high rises was lined with shopping carts carrying the people's lives who crowded under it, looking for relief from

the sun until they were chased away by security guards.

Out of the scavenged piles along their path, one stuck out. There were two refrigerator boxes stacked on top of each other, covered by a tattered blue tarp. A clothes washer box sat on either side layered over with rags from waterproof clothes, carefully duct taped together to shield them from the rain.

While the size of the shelter and efforts to preserve it made it stand out, that was not what drew the most attention. The opening of every box had things spilling out of it. The box on the left had a pile of food spilling out of it-partially emptied chip bags, different kinds of fruit starting to go bad, and other snacks in various states of disrepair. The container on the right had clothing sneaking out the door-underwear, coats, jeans, shirts and shoes of various sizes and colors. The main box in the back showed the ends of several blankets and a couple pillows trying to escape.

A handful of men loitered on the sidewalk under the meager shade of the porticos of the building beside the shelter. Some leaned listlessly against the side, seemingly oblivious to the world passing them by. The rest stood in a loose group, talking amongst themselves and engaging those who entered their territory with creative pleas for either jobs or donations. Their panhandling had become somewhat strident after a long day in the stifling heat with few targets for their pitches.

One of the more outgoing men spotted the group standing in front of the cardboard palace. Tall and muscular with a full head of grizzled hair, his quick wit and positive attitude pushed back against the oppressive heat and poverty. "Hey now gents, you best be moving along," he said. "If Hoarder Hessie catches you eyeballing her stuff there's no telling what she will do," he warned. "She might invite you in for a bite to eat, or chase you off with her machete, depending on her mood."

"Now George, you hush your mouth." The thin, reedy voice punched out of the smog to confront the person who dared reveal the identity of the person stealthily watching the group from the darkness inside. "You just go on and mind your own business. I can take care of myself."

"That you can, Hessie." George said with a laugh as he turned back to his friends. After he turned, he muttered under his breath, "You aren't the one I'm worried about."

"So what's it going to be, Hessie?" The leader of the group spoke into the shadows. "Are you going to chase us off, or are you going to let your curiosity run free?"

"Oh, all right, come here," Hessie said. "Don't have room for all of you to come in so we'll have to chat outside. Too many of you to eat more than some crackers, either."

Jesus stepped up to the front of the tent as the blankets moved far enough apart for the mysterious woman inside to come out. Somewhere around five feet tall with drooping shoulders and a pronounced limp, she was wearing clothes that matched her personality. Her blouse was covered with large black flowers against a purple background, which contrasted violently with the baggy fluorescent orange shorts covering most of her tea-brown legs. Her straggly hair poofed out randomly from underneath a purple crocheted hat shoved jauntily over her head.

Hessie opened four small packages of cheese and crackers with slightly dented ends and distributed the contents to the group. "Ain't got much, but I share what I have with my friends," she said. Now, why are you here talking to me instead of being in one of those fancy churches preaching?

Jesus gave a small laugh. "So you know who I am, then. Well, we were walking over to the park to talk to people there, but I had to bring you this." With that he reached into his pocket and pulled out a small porcelain statue of Moses with the Ten Commandments held to his side by one hand while the other held his staff over his head.

Hessie looked at him in awe. "Where did you get that," she asked with a tremor in her voice. "I didn't think they existed anymore."

Jesus handed it to her and smiled. "Well, I have some pretty good sources. One of them told me you have been praying for one of these for years."

"I have been," Hessie answered. "I have had every figure in this set for decades, except for this one. I have had to give up many things, but I always kept this collection hoping to finish it. How can I thank you for this generous gift?"

"Just keep doing what you do best," Jesus replied. "Scare away those who cause trouble and help those who need it the most. You don't have any idea how many lives you've impacted from your cardboard palace here."

Hessie's face broke out into a big smile. "I will do that, sir. I will help out those who come my way and tell them your story."

Jesus stood up, and the disciples followed his example. "Thank you for the crackers. Before we go on, I will help your efforts a little more." With that he moved over to the pile of food and said a short blessing over it. He gave her a final salute, then started down the street again.

As they passed the men in front of the building, George couldn't help commenting on what happened. "Hey now. I haven't seen her react like that to anyone in a long time. What kind of magic did you use on her?

"No magic, George." Jesus answered. "Just answered a prayer she has been making for about twenty years. I think you will find she will be quite chipper now."

George looked at him with a wry smile on his face. "Well, good for her," he said. "She deserves it. Just wish someone would answer a few more prayers for the people around here." With that he started turning back to his friends.

"One more thing, George," Jesus said.

George turned back towards him. "Yes," he asked? "Don't tell me you are going to pull another rabbit out of your hat."

"No rabbits in this hat," Jesus said as he raised his battered Cubs cap briefly. "But I did hear that the Holy Name Cathedral just lost their maintenance supervisor. Somehow your name came up in the discussion of who to replace him. If you were to go over there today with a couple of your hard-working friends,

I think some more prayers will be answered today. That is, if you can spare the time from keeping Hessie in line."

"I don't know how you heard that, but I'll take anything right now." George said. "This is crazy, but somehow I believe you. Jim, Hosea, come on. If we leave now we can make it before everyone quits for the day. Let's go."

"Not without something to drink." Hessie was standing behind them with three bottles of water. "I thought I only had one left, but there are more where that came from. Don't suppose you know anything about that, now would you," she asked Jesus as she gave them the bottles.

Jesus just grinned at her. They made their final farewells, and they all headed out towards their destinations.

After walking past a few more makeshift shelters the sound of sing-song voices began to rise above the tires thumping over potholes and the roar of frustrated air conditioners. The tune was vague at first but became more recognizable the closer they came to the next alley.

"Why Jesus, I do believe they are singing your tune," James said as they came to the mouth of the alley. Two teenage girls stood just inside, arms and legs covered in sores and high as a kite, slowly dancing to their own rendition of "Jesus Loves Me."

Too caught up in their own small world of chemical euphoria to notice them at first, the girls continued singing and dancing with the thin shadows they cast. John coughed against the misty dirt, which drew their attention away from their inner demons to the men watching them.

"Hey there, honey, want to have a good time," one of them asked? "It will only cost you five dollars."

"No thank you, you're too beautiful for me," Jesus answered. That was so unexpected it partially pushed the fog away from their brain to focus on who was talking to them.

After a pause, the other girl snorted and asked, "Are you looking at a picture on your phone, or are you just drunk?"

"Oh, just remembering what you used to look like before you stuck the first needle in your arm," Jesus said. "With the looks of a model and a firm belief in who you were singing about, how did you come to this?"

"Just trying to make a living until I get that role in the theatre," she said. "Fat chance of that happening now, although I have gotten paid for a few jobs in the movie theater."

"Just not the kind you were hoping for, right," Jesus asked? "If this is all you have now, why do you still sing to Him?"

"He is all I have left," she responded. "I keep hoping some-day He will come and pull me out of this life."

Jesus walked up to them and put a hand on each of their shoulders.

"Oh honey, both of us," she asked? "I don't need any help to make you happy."

"No, nothing like that," Jesus said. "Today your prayers have been answered." With that he told their demons of addiction to leave. With cries of protest and a few contortions the girl's bodies came to rest, their eyes and minds clear for the first time in months.

"Thank you," they said over and over again. "Who are you?"

"I am the one you were singing to," Jesus answered. "Now go to the mission and they will help you get back home. Your parents and the life you once wanted are waiting for you there."

The girls headed to the mission and once again began singing "Jesus Loves Me" with renewed energy and meaning. The disciples continued down Monroe again. The breeze picked up a little as the afternoon wore on, easing the heat and chasing the humidity away slightly faster than it collected on your skin.

As they approached the intersection with Columbus Drive, the number of homeless on the sidewalk increased. The ones closest to the corner ran out with every light change trying to earn a buck by washing windshields. Those on the curb shook cans at the cars waiting for the light to change. Others leaned against the skyscrapers on one side and trees in the park on the other, holding up signs and calling out to the business-men running between buildings They turned left on the far side of the road and wove their way between shopping carts and people positioning themselves for the most donations. There was plenty of misery on display here, some of which was magnified with makeup and props to increase the pity factor. Jesus greeted everyone they met, but none of this group caught his attention.

They turned right when they reached Randolph Street. A few of the homeless sought shelter in Maggie Daley Park under the trees and in the flower gardens until the police rousted them. As they came closer to the intersection with Lake Shore Drive the homeless population disappeared, driven under the overpasses during the day so the Columbia Yacht Club members on the other side of the highway would not be distracted or embarrassed by their proximity.

Peanut Park itself was a disappointment. Once full of trees and bushes, the only greenery in site was grass on one side and new tennis courts on the other. Not only had all the shade been removed to discourage any squatters, but regular patrols made sure the office workers would not be disturbed as they came to get some exercise during the day. The only thing left in the park that benefited those living in the shadows was the locker rooms for the tennis courts, where they could sneak in after midnight for a real shower-if they had someone with them they could trust to watch their things. Even though part of the goal of the tennis courts was to drive the homeless away from this area of urban renewal, all it did was pack more people into smaller spaces under the overpasses. Crime went up outside the small oasis of new buildings, making the areas on either side more dangerous instead of safer.

"Let's go to the coffee house across the street and wait until it gets dark," Jesus said. "That is when they will start migrating back into the park. There are still a couple people I need to talk to. Until then we will see if there is anyone over there that is interested in a conversation more than the numbers on their computer."

With that they entered the coffee shop and took over the

one large table in the back. With a round of drinks and sand-wiches they settled back into the chairs and began examining the customers as they came in for their breaks. After the length-ening shadows began drawing the homeless out from their shel-ters into the park, Jesus and his disciples threw away their trash, to find the ones they had come looking for.

Reflections

1 Corinthians 4:11 To this very hour we go hungry and thirsty, we are in rags, we are brutally treated, we are homeless.

Homelessness is a tricky topic to deal with. The number of homeless in an area is related more to population density than it is to economic condition. This may seem outrageous to some, but poverty tends to concentrate in areas with other issues-drug and alcohol abuse, crime, cultures embedded with beliefs which deter success and high costs of living. People with limited income in rural areas tend to have better success not only because lower costs of living allows their money to go fur-ther, but people in those areas typically look out for each other and find ways to care for those who struggle.

Another consistent factor with homelessness is mental illness. This can manifest in many ways, all of which contrib-ute to their economic conditions. Some mental illnesses, such as PTSD and hallucinations, cause their victims to isolate them-selves from society. Other mental illnesses cause concentration issues which prevent their victims from working long hours.

A third factor common to homelessness is economic in-security. This is not so much a personal condition as a cultural one. Businesses do not invest in areas with high crime rates not only to properties, but also where potential customers are at risk coming to them. High permit fees and tax rates combined with high rents in dilapidated buildings also discourage busi-nesses from expanding in depressed urban areas.

Questions for Contemplation

1. Does your community have a homelessness issue? If so, what are the main issues driving the problem?

2. Do you believe there is a religious root to the homelessness issue? If so, what is it and how can it be addressed?

3. Several of the social issues behind being homeless have religious aspects to them. There are demonic influences in drug abuse and cultures of violence for example. What role can churches and community groups play in reversing these aspects of homelessness?

4. A key to disrupting the cycle of urban homelessness is direct intervention. This is best accomplished through direct mentoring, which can take the form of community sports organizations or tutoring programs. How can you personally reach out to break the cycle of hopelessness in your local area?

5. Providing opportunities for those looking for them is important in breaking the cycle of poverty. Are there home-based or co-op businesses in your area who would be able to train the homeless in your area who

are not already working?

Call to Action

There are many small ways you can address homelessness. The first way is to treat someone who is homeless the same way you would treat anyone else. Smile at them and take the time to exchange small talk. Being treated like an ordinary person can do wonders for the emotional state of someone who has been treated poorly.

If God leads you, help them out. This isn't necessarily by handing someone money, although that is a possibility. If they say they are hungry, take them somewhere and eat a meal with them. If they say they need food, take them to the grocery store. This allows you to give them your personal attention, but it provides them with basic needs.

If you can, take them into your business and train them with the skills they need to work. If you know of programs that will assist them with food, clothing or work write down how to contact them. Invite them to church. Again, treat them like a neighbor.

For an index of homeless shelters you can go to https://www.homelessshelterdirectory.org/. Contact your church to find out more about who to contact for assistance with rides, food, clothes and bills. Most of all, volunteer at local shelters, outreach programs, tutoring programs and training classes to have a direct influence. Praying is helpful, but it takes people to make a difference in someone's life.

4. BURNING MAN

The throbbing mass of humanity in Black Rock City focused on the Burners with their torches dancing around the Temple of Whollyness. The sixty-four-foot pyramid of interlocking wooden puzzle pieces anchored in smaller pyramids at the corners flickered in the torchlight. Shadows fought as the dancers weaved their way around the structure, creeping up the sides as their patterns drew them closer to the base. When they were within a few feet of the building they circled it seven times to complete their mockery of the fairy tale god. The drums swelled in crescendo, then stopped. On cue the crowd shouted, and the Burners threw their torches into its open arches. Flames rapidly enveloped the base, then raced up the inside walls.

The Burners joined the crowd and watched in silence as flames roared through their temporary house of worship. Tears glistened in many eyes, and some began sobbing as the scribbled notes of loss and remorse tacked onto the walls were devoured by the flames. The artificial space created to bring temporary relief and focus to those who only worship themselves quickly went from wood to flame to a smoldering pile of ashes. Their appeals to the divine in themselves were gone, and the societal sadness and remorse from the past year held their attention long after the flames died down.

The crowd shrank rapidly after the last beams collapsed into the heap of ashes outlining the borders of the temple. The incoming chill of the desert night air chased those on the outskirts back to their miniature neighborhoods. On this night of the festival, many would forego a night of unbridled revelry to quietly reflect on the events of their last year. Several stayed to watch the embers wink out, seeing their identities in the wood as it flamed for a time before dying into nothingness. A few tortured souls stayed on, moving ever closer to the diminishing pile of lost hope and beauty, drawn like moths to the light but unable to take the final step of proving their lack of spiritual being by joining the seething mass of embers.

Only the center of the former temple continued glowing as midnight approached. A dozen people remained in a loose formation, their desire for silent solitude overcome by the need for warmth and human comfort. Fierce forts of self-made independence forced to deal with their inadequate humanness, the longing for a greater meaning pinned them to the fire consuming the last admittance of weakness they would allow themselves.

A stranger moved out of the shadows and walked purposefully into the group. Everyone shifted uneasily at his casual intrusion into the closest thing they had to the sacred. As some turned to leave, the stranger addressed them.

"You are all here because you suffered significant losses this year. Some of you have lost spouses and partners. Others have lost jobs. Most of you faced the death of someone close to you. No matter what the loss was, you are convinced your loss is permanent.

When you believe everything happens by accident, and you are responsible for creating everything in this world, this also gives you the overwhelming responsibility for causing the destruction of what you make. If you created a family, you are responsible for it falling apart. If you created a relationship, its failure is your responsibility. If you created a career, you ultimately caused it to fall apart. If you created a financial empire, you are responsible for its collapse. Whatever is created will eventually be destroyed, and you are responsible either way.

In many aspects this is true. Even with the most meticulous planning, everyone makes mistakes. Those mistakes have consequences you cannot foresee, which can destroy everything you have worked for. Simply choosing to stand here in the cold desert air will lead to death for one of you, so some of those choices which seem insignificant in the moment have great consequences.

I have good news for you, though. None of you are accidents. There is a God, and he created you to fill important roles in this life. Not only that but he cares about each one of you in the everyday things that happen in your lives. There is life after death, and you have the hope of being reunited with those you lost.

You are all at the end of your ropes in one way or another. Tonight, you have a choice. Are you going to continue to cling to a belief you are all there is, or are you going to accept the gnawing hope in you that calls out for a God that loves and cares for you? Is this going to be the end of your dream, or are you going to reach out past yourself to the one who created you? You can begrudgingly accept the end of your dreams or accept the help of the One who created the dream in you.

If you truly believe you are all there is, go back to your beds so you can toss and turn all night trying to figure out how to turn your defeat back into victory. If you want to accept the hope and power of someone bigger than yourself, then I will show you a more excellent way. The choice is yours."

With that he fell silent, waiting. Half the group hurried away from the stranger who dared challenge their arrogance and way of life. The other half gathered around the stranger, who began telling them of the hope they had in front of them. Each group chose their future path, but some left with new hope and understanding.

Reflection

Psalm 14:1 The fool says in his heart, "There is no God." They are corrupt, their deeds are vile; there is no one who does good.

Every year there is a festival called "Burning Man" in the Nevada desert. It is the ultimate celebration of hedonism, attended mainly by atheists and hippies to celebrate humans and

their accomplishments in arts, government and other areas. It is a community built on the premise that man is God and celebrates his accomplishments. All goods and services are bartered, and each part of the community is built around a theme celebrating a part of humanism. A giant effigy of a man is built which is burned on the last night as the grand finale of partying.

Each year they also build a temple whose name is a pun of the Christian god, who they don't believe in. It is a monument to human ego, and throughout the celebration people fasten notes to the wall about the highlights and failures they had during the year. One night the temple is burned in an anti-religious ceremony signifying whatever happened is over, and it is an emotional experience for the community.

Questions for Contemplation

1. Burning failures in a temple is based on the same concept of tearing up a sheet of paper with your failures on it. It is a good therapy technique, but only affects your thinking about the situation. Do you think doing something like this as an epic ritual is more effective?

2. What are the differences between believing you are ultimately responsible for everything you do and having a God that has an ultimate plan for your life?

3. How does hopelessness play a role in someone who does not believe there is a God who provides freedom through forgiveness and the possibility of divine intervention to improve situations in life?

4. What ways can desperate situations open the door to reaching people who have rejected God in the past?

5. There are many reasons people quit believing in God. Some believe they are too smart, but many trace their disbelief back to where they trusted God for help in a desperate situation that didn't turn out the way they wanted. Is there any way you can think of to reach out to someone who has rejected God because of unanswered prayers?

Call to Action

Many people think they can reach atheists by reasoning with them. This approach usually fails, essentially because Christianity is based on what someone who rejects God considers foolishness. The average person can spend hours arguing with an atheist without making a dint in their beliefs. There are a rare few with the depth of knowledge and experience who can reach them from a rational aspect, such as Ravi Zacharias at RZIM.org.

The most effective way for someone who isn't a theological genius to reach an atheist is to follow Christ. Be the extraordinary person who shows the fruits of the spirit. Have the courage to allow Holy Spirit to use them to perform miracles. Be a shining light instead of trying to be a flaming sword. When an atheist begins searching to fill the emptiness they feel, they will be attracted to someone who genuinely shines God's light to the world.

5. THE UNIT

The waiting room outside the Neonatal Intensive Care Unit (NICU) in Morgantown, West Virginia began to form at 8:30 AM. It is a part of the J. W. Ruby Memorial Hospital on the campus of West Virginia University. Originally funded by donations from his estate, the hospital is the flagship of the West Virginia School of Medicine.

The most common reason babies end up here are their mothers are in their early teens and not physically developed enough to have a healthy pregnancy. The next leading reason is their mothers are addicted to drugs, which causes birth defects. The smallest fraction of patients are babies with medical issues from healthy and mature mothers.

The unit serves a rural area with thirty nine beds. Only two people are allowed into the unit per child, and many of the teenage mothers were still asleep. Visitors are not allowed to stay overnight to give the babies time to sleep, although they are still given treatments. The enforced rest time is as much for the new mothers as it is for the babies. That is a two-edged sword, however. Hotels in the area are expensive since it is a college town, so some of the families travel two or more hours each way to the hospital every day to be with their children.

When everyone was checked in and it was 9:00 AM, the doors opened and the visitors were allowed inside. One of the rules of the unit is you are only supposed to pay attention to your own patient. The unit is relatively dark, without overhead lights. Each incubator is lit with natural light bulbs to simulate the sun and help the babies produce Vitamin D. Privacy curtains line the outside of the incubators, but a quick glance inside typically shows a severely underweight infant with transparent skin and IVs and breathing tubes in them. There are lots of monitors and blinking lights, but most of the machines are muted to give the babies as much rest as possible. One thing that can't be muted is the steady, rapid poofs of air sent by the respirators into their underdeveloped lungs.

The medical condition of a neonate can change rapidly, and treatments are smaller and more frequent. There is one nurse for every two babies to monitor them and give them their treatments when scheduled. Dressed in scrubs like other nurses, their jobs are not just focused on caring for their patients. They also have to make sure the visitors follow all of the rules and help teach them how to care for their babies as well. Part nurse and part mother, a shift can go from comforter to chaos in seconds.

Tania and Fred Stillwell walked slowly between the rows of incubators to where their baby Henry lay in the back of the room. They both snuck glances at the other babies as they passed, their tiny translucent bodies freshly diapered and shining from lotions to keep their skin moist. Most had tubes connected to them through their belly buttons, and they were barely visible between the machines on the side of the incubator. Others were only connected to the respirator, and light spilled out from the sides of their units.

Henry was one of the lucky ones. Tania was in her thirties and had a relatively normal pregnancy. His lungs were slightly underdeveloped, though, so he needed help breathing for a couple weeks until they were able to function fully on their own. His skin was normal, and he would have been able to drink from a bottle if he did not have to have a breathing tube down his throat. His condition was normal and stable outside of his breathing issues.

Tania longed to pick up Henry and hold him, but all babies had to remain in their incubator until they were developed enough to tolerate being held. The two key elements of reaching that stage were being able to breathe on their own and hold their temperature outside of the incubator. Only one person could reach into the incubator at a time, so she reached in and firmly gripped his hand as he made a fist. She could not even caress his face since light touches made him recoil in fear. He opened his fist enough she was able to slide her finger inside it, and they stayed like that until he stretched and released it. Her arm was tired from reaching into the unit so she rested as Fred took his turn giving parental comfort to Henry. They both talked to Henry, but their voices were hushed following another rule to prevent startling any of the patients.

The relative quiet of the room was disrupted when Finley entered the room, her case worker close behind. Her baby was the other patient Henry's nurse took care of, so they had gotten to know each other in the few days they had been there. She was only fifteen, and her baby Mason was severely underdeveloped since he was born six weeks early. He was only three pounds two ounces at birth and struggled to gain weight. Not only was he on a ventilator, he had an IV coming out of his umbilical cord since his arms and legs were too small to handle it. A surgery was scheduled the next day to repair a hole in his heart, which would allow him to start growing easier.

Finley had hidden her pregnancy from her parents, and they still didn't know she had had a baby. She was still going to school to make things as normal as possible, so she could only see her baby on evenings and weekends. Her social worker would show up frequently, trying to convince her to be with her baby more often. She also tried to convince her to let her parents know what was going on so they could help her with the baby, and plan for taking care of him when he was released. So far she hadn't been successful with either endeavor, but not from a lack of trying.

When it was noon, all the visitors had to leave the NICU. The nurses had an hour to give their two charges their treatments, take vital signs and any necessary lab tests, change, and clean them. While the visitors were reluctant to leave, three hours by the incubator seems to grow longer as their baby stays there. Tania and Fred started taking books with them to read

while the other person took their turn. Then there were the frequent times when Henry slept and they both had to entertain themselves. They kept track of how he was progressing with the nurse and doctors, but even that could only fill so much of their time. Everyone had to take all of their belongings with them each break to give the nurses enough room to work.

As they walked out, Finley followed them down the hall to the elevator. Her social worker temporarily stopped pursuing her to talk with another parent on her list. She looked exhausted, not only from running back and forth to the hospital but from the constant battle she fought with her social worker and her decisions for the future.

They invited Finley to go with them, since it looked like she could use someone different to talk to. She agreed, glad to talk to someone else going through the same experience. They decided to stay at the hospital for lunch to avoid fighting the traffic with the students and businesses nearby. Besides, the prices were hard to beat and the food was not bad, either.

There were four men standing by the elevator when they reached it, so their conversation turned to the weather and general baby stuff. Their hesitancy did not last long when the one with the long hair and beard pulled out an oversized raccoon rattle. They had been in the step down unit to see the one called Harry's son, who had graduated from NICU two weeks earlier. He began acting like Harry's arm was the crib, making odd noises as he compared the big rattle to the little tiny baby. The toy had been banned from the unit because of its size, but it did make for some amusing comparisons.

The one joking around turned out to be Jesus, the leader. The other two were James and Thomas. All three of them looked a little rough, their jeans and polos contrasting with Harry's suit. Their relaxed joking soon drew Tania, Fred and Finley into engaging as well by the time they entered the elevator. When they all got off on the same floor and headed the same direction, eating together seemed to be the natural thing to do.

They wandered through the line. The options were

limited, and they ended up with two salads, two hamburgers and two fish specials. Jesus insisted on paying for all of their meals, which they appreciated. They raided the condiment table, then took over the large table by the window. It was quiet for several minutes while they dug into their meals, quiet enough to hear the two nurses on the other side of the room complaining about a patient who constantly rang her buzzer for things she could do herself.

The complaints about the patient's complaints quickly became annoying. Suddenly Jesus pulled out the raccoon rattle and had it start trying to eat French fries. Nobody could keep a straight face with the great sincerity and difficulty it had trying to eat. The fries were not well cooked, and the limp fry fell away from its mouth every time he tried lifting it with its tiny arms.

With the silence broken again, the conversation turned back towards the babies and the unique struggles they faced. Harry's son Nolan was about to be released to the "real world," and they were getting a quick bite while the nurses finished their prep work and packing. Henry's lungs were reaching full development, but they expected it to take another week. Finley told about her family not knowing she was pregnant, and the strong disapproval they had for anyone having a baby out of wedlock.

Most of the conversation focused on Finley and how she should deal with her family. They encouraged her to let them know what was going on and trust them to love and accept Mason. They shared some resources she could get help from that the social worker didn't know about, and gave her some contacts in her own church who had gone through similar situations.

Time passed quickly, and it was one o'clock before they knew it. Harry's phone buzzed and his wife Georgia told him everything was ready for them to leave. Jesus sent up a quick prayer for all babies, blessing each one. Harry grabbed a coffee and sandwich for Georgia and headed back upstairs with the rest of the group in tow. It took a few tries for the raccoon to successfully push the right button, but they were soon on the way back up to the NICU and step down units.

As they got off the elevator, Fred noticed someone pacing at the end of the hallway. He motioned to Jesus, who smiled and nodded at him. Finley had her head down, trying to avoid her case worker if she was around. Jesus gently pulled her aside in that direction as if to give her a last piece of advice. As she talked to hm, she glanced over his shoulder and saw the woman pacing. She gasped and tried to step behind him. The woman was watching the group, and started walking towards them

It was Finley's Mom, and she ran to her daughter. That morning while she was having her devotions, she had spent extra time praying for her daughter and her strange behavior recently. She felt a sudden urge to go to the hospital right then. Once she was there her finger pushed the button for the sixth floor. She had only been there a few minutes, but she had gone to the end of the hallway to pray, trying to figure out why she was there. Now she knew.

Fred's group turned towards the step down unit, ready to pick up Nolan. They didn't make it very far, though. As soon as Harry stepped in front of the waiting room door it burst open. The volunteer Grandma who had helped them pushed her way through the door, one of their bags in each hand. Mom came next, with one of the nurses whispering reminders and encouragement in her ear. By the time Mom was out of the door with Nolan, Grandma had handed the bags to Thomas and was leading the group back to the elevator. She pushed the button to the ground floor and waved at Jesus to hurry as he was making his way from the other end of the hallway.

Tania and Fred had stopped in front of the NICU waiting room door to watch the spectacle. As he walked past them, Jesus touched their shoulders to get their attention.

"It won't be long now," Jesus said. "As soon as they clean out Nolan's incubator, they will move Henry into it."

Just then the elevator opened, and the nurse and Grandma

fussed at the group to get in. Mom had to get in first, and Dad made a production of making sure everyone got on without crowding the baby. The doors started to close while everyone was still shifting around. The rattle was almost a casualty though, as it stuck out under Jesus' arm far enough the door alarm was triggered and they reopened. Everyone laughed as he switched positions so it hung safely down in front of him. The door closed, and the hallway suddenly became very quiet.

The nurse and volunteer Grandma gave each other a high five, then started walking back to their unit. The show was over, so Fred opened the door to the NICU. They were anxious to get back to Henry, and they were both curious about what Jesus had just told them. Curious, but jaded by the hurry up and wait routine, they buzzed the unit door for a nurse to let them in.

Their hearts sank as they walked toward Henry's incubator. There were two nurses and a doctor huddled over him, talking and making notes. It usually wasn't a good sign when this happened, especially when the time for treatments was over. They seemed to be making some adjustments as well.

When they came close enough for the doctor to see them, he motioned them over. The nurses kept doing whatever it was they were up to, but it looked like they were smiling.

"Don't look so nervous," Dr. Maki said. "Henry's lungs have developed enough to be taken off the breathing tube. We are just watching him to make sure his vital signs are stable without them. If everything stays stable, we will move him to the step down unit as soon as they are ready for him."

It seemed Jesus knew what was going on the whole time. Moving into the step down unit meant Henry was one step closer to going home. They would be able to hold him, since he would tolerate more physical touch. He would still be on oxygen for a few days, but he would not have as many treatments. Someone could be with him all the time, and more visitors could come see him as well. Life was one step closer to being normal again. Well, as normal as a new baby would permit, at least.

Reflections:

Mark 9:37"Whoever welcomes one of these little children in my name welcomes me; and whoever welcomes me does not welcome me but the one who sent me."

This story is based on the experience of Tara Quigley, who shared her and her husband Joe's experience with their son in the NICU. I appreciate her sharing her experiences with me in to make it possible.

Babies are the bundles of joy almost everyone enjoys being around. Even if people don't want to have kids of their own, most of them like to spend time around them. The newness of life and journey of learning about the things around them holds a special fascination. Even when they become fountains of vomit or have gag worthy bowel movements, they are things to celebrate and brag about instead of generating disgust.

Having a baby disrupts life in the most perfect families. Waking up every couple of hours demanding to be fed and crying constantly for reasons you do not understand makes life difficult. When they get sick it is even worse, and frequent vomiting and diarrhea can become life threatening. Trips to the doctor for checkups and vaccines can play havoc with work schedules. Even if insurance covers most of the costs of their birth and checkups, the cost of feeding and clothing a baby on top of buying them furniture, car seats and toys takes some adjusting to.

Just having a baby is life changing. But what if that baby changed your whole life? What if that baby needed constant monitoring? What if they could not breathe on their own because their lungs weren't developed enough? What if they could not eat because their stomach wasn't ready for food? What if they are addicted to drugs, and those drugs have caused birth defects that have to be corrected by multiple surgeries? What if those birth defects affect their brains so they will never be able to be considered "normal?"

If your baby turns out to fit in one of those categories, they will have to spend time in a Neonatal Intensive Care Unit (NICU). The equipment and specialized care is expensive. If they must have surgeries, the bills keep piling up. Once they can leave the NICU they go to the step-down unit, which costs less but still has the expenses of specialized care and equipment. The more advanced babies can just spend a couple weeks in the step-down unit, while those who are extremely premature or have severe health issues can take several months before they are ready to be released.

What does your life look like as a parent? If both parents are present and working, at least one of them usually makes the hard decision to quit while the other one maxes out their sick leave to take care of their baby and family. The self-employed often must shut down their businesses until the baby is at least stable. The bills skyrocket as their income decreases or stops. Insurance deductibles and travel and hotel expenses keep building up as caring for their baby takes precedence over everything else.

Questions for Contemplation:

1. Christians are famous for preaching about family coming second only to God. Most are ok with parents taking time off for a few days to take care of a child who is sick or has been injured. Would you be as sympathetic with a family who gives up their income for months to care for a premature baby?

2. Life essentially stops for a family with a baby in NICU. They do not need help with one thing, they need help with everything. Money for travel and eating out is

important. So is money to cover their rent or mortgage, utilities, insurance premiums and deductibles. What are some ways you and your church could help cover these expenses in meaningful ways?

3. A baby in the NICU can be especially devastating if there are other children in the family. While caring for the baby takes an immense amount of time, the needs of the other children can't be neglected. They have school to go to, homework to do, and meals and bedtime schedules to keep. What ways can you and your church assist the family in crisis to keep their family from falling apart?

4. Babies have a higher risk of ending up in the NICU if their mothers are in a high risk group. The highest risk group is unwed teenagers, ages sixteen and below. The second highest risk group is drug and alcohol addicts. What stigmas do Christians attach to these groups that make them reluctant to engage with them? What should we do to overcome those stigmas?

5. Some Christians believe diseases and illnesses are a judgement from God for sin. They would assume a premature baby is the result of some sin by one or both parents. Even if the family is someone they have known for many years with an excellent reputation,

it would be a sign to them of something dark and shameful in their past. They would show concern for the baby, but eventually grill the parents to try to get them to confess their sins so the baby can heal faster. If someone you know has a premature baby and confides in you this is happening to them, what are some ways you can intervene in the situation to end the suspicion and accusations?

Call to Action:

Over eleven percent of all births are premature. That averages around four hundred fifty thousand in the United States alone. Babies born before they are twenty-three weeks old aren't treated, because they rarely survive. The cost of caring for a premature baby averages three thousand dollars a day and can be significantly higher if they undergo multiple surgeries.

While it seems like there are a lot of premature babies, most towns rarely see one. Because of this, it is difficult for churches or communities to develop programs to help them specifically. There are hot spots for preemies, though, which are typically urban non-white communities with high numbers of teenage pregnancies, single parent homes and drug abuse where they happen frequently enough that it makes sense for churches to develop ongoing programs for them.

Most programs to help families with premature babies are developed around the hospitals with NICU units. The hospitals develop teams of doctors, nurses, and aides to assist with their medical care in the hospital. They also help coordinate volunteer Grandmas, social workers, and support groups to help them handle their demands.

The March of Dimes has a program called The Prematurity Campaign. Most of their efforts go towards finding the causes of premature births and preventing them. They do have the capability to help families after birth, but you must contact them for specific details.

Miracle Babies is a program in San Diego, California dedicated to helping families through the entire preemie experience. This runs the gamut from financial assistance with supplies to educational programs on the different aspects of care. They have a limited service area but could be a good resource on where to find assistance in other locations.

When a premature birth happens in your church or community, be the one to start organizing assistance for them. Do it within hours, not days or weeks. Usually there is some group in a church focused on caring for those in need, but the urgency of this situation is usually overwhelming. If the family is too far from the NICU hospital to come home every day, the focus should be on gift cards and monetary donations to cover food and travel. If they are close, they still need food and travel expenses during the day but can use families bringing cooked meals to them in the evening as they will be stressed and exhausted. If they have other children, they need volunteers to care for and feed them, along with getting them to activities and doing homework.

The needs of caring for a premature baby are usually unexpected, takes up all your time, and is financially demanding. The good news is, they usually develop enough so they can go home in a couple weeks. Unfortunately, the experience can last for months if the baby is extremely young or has severe health issues, so they may need assistance for an extended amount of time. The need here is not one of organizing a program or educating others as much as being prepared to act immediately if this type of situation arises.

6. NORTH POINT CHURCH

The board room in the Executive Suite of North Point hummed with anticipation. The pre-service meeting was usually reserved for Ministry Team leaders, but today the massive room enclosed in real oak paneling was crowded with guests as well. The wi-fi workstations built into the contemporary conference table hummed with matching I-Pads as the head of the worship team scrolled through the order of service, making sure everyone knew their cues so everything would move seamlessly in the tight live TV and internet broadcasts. They each had a beeper to cue them five minutes before they were due up, coordinated from the massive production studio hovering above the balcony in the back.

The pre-service meeting used to be a time for the leaders to pray for the service with a quick review of the day's plan. However, as the congregation grew, more "stuff" was added to get people involved and entertained. Professionals were hired to ensure the highest quality of "stuff" was being shared, which led to more ego conflicts and the need for a tight schedule to keep everyone in line. As the service grew more complex, more and more time had to be devoted to scheduling-leaving less and less time for prayer. Guests, of course, made this even worse. Instead of individuals pouring out their heart, now the lead pastor offered a short platitude at the end accompanied by the restless shifting of people in a hurry to get to their designated spots before the service started.

The guests that morning came for two very different reasons. The first guest, squeezed in for five minutes at the beginning of the service (while many people would still be in the lobby or distracted looking for seats) was there to update the church on the community sports team he had started in one of the rougher neighborhoods of Atlanta. Participant numbers were growing, and the outreach was starting to affect the community to the point crime and truancy rates had started to drop. As the number of participants grew, so did the need for more funds to have adequate equipment and to start satellite groups in other locations. The leader had asked for fifteen minutes to not only present the results and needs, but to also have a couple of the participants share their stories. Time was short that morning (even with cutting out a song!) so five minutes was all they could give him.

The second set of guests contrasted with the first. They were business leaders who would be recognized for their large contributions to the just-completed sanctuary overhaul. Not only was the latest technology available in the boardroom, it was all over the sanctuary as well. Earpieces could be checked out at the welcome centers for translations into several different languages. I-Pads that clipped onto the back of pews were available for the hearing impaired. All over the cavernous sanctuary (and lobby and children's church check-in) screens passed along information from the projector screens as surround sound speakers pumped out music from the digital sound board. The smart lights and multi-layered stage added dimensions to the presentation once it was underway. Yes, from a technological standpoint, the church was perfect.

As the meeting ended, the first guest tried to network directly with the business leaders for resources. Since he was scheduled at the beginning, he was whisked away to his designated seat immediately. The businessmen milled around, getting coffee refills and more pastries, which meant most of them wouldn't be in position to hear about the ministry outreach.

Everything was operating exactly as planned, and all was right in the world. Until the businessmen entered the sanctuary to take their seats, that is. As the music faded and the outreach leader began to speak, the businessmen's escort abruptly halted their progress and confusion reigned because of an epic failure by the ushers. For there, in the front row reserved for the big donors, sat thirteen men in jeans and polo shirts.

This was a disaster of epic proportion. First, that the ushers had allowed the general public to sit in reserved seats. Second, that anyone not in formal dress would sit close enough to the platform they could be seen as the cameras filmed the activities on stage. And, last but not least, that it would be basically impossible to remove the group without at least some of the action showing up on camera.

As fire came down the line from the welcoming committee/ushers to those responsible for that section, nobody remembered the group walking down the aisle and entering the spit-shined reserved seating. The group was listening intently to the outreach report, so focused nobody seemed to have the courage to approach the group to relocate them-outside of the church, if at all possible.

Seeing nothing happening, the chair of the welcoming committee headed down the aisle at full steam. Just before reaching the top of the section, the outreach report finished. When it concluded the offending group rose in unison and began walking down the aisle to the exit. They were quickly surrounded by security, who escorted them out of the sanctuary. Two ushers quickly spot cleaned the seats before giving the all clear signal to the donor's escorts, who seated the businessmen as planned so the show could go on as scheduled.

When the deposed group reached a quiet spot in the hallway, the chair abruptly stopped and turned to face the offenders. He was breathing heavily, and his nose flared with each exhalation. He squinted his eyes at them in a look that he obviously practiced to intimidate others, but which came across more like suppressed bewilderment.

"What were you doing, sitting in the reserved area," he huffed. The thought of introducing himself to these strangers never crossed his mind.

"Well, David," the leader answered, "I didn't realize the flashing red pictures on the end of the aisle meant they were re-

served. "

"I'm not sure how you could have missed it, since the seating codes cycle through the announcements on the screen every three minutes." David replied. He felt it was beneath his office and the situation to find out how this stranger knew his name or find out what his was.

"I'm sorry, I was more interested in what your outreach group is doing than watching your ads," Jesus answered. "Did you even listen to his story?"

"I don't have time to listen to anything until everyone gets settled," David sniffed. "I am responsible to make sure everyone gets settled before the TV cameras start panning the audience. Now why did you decide to create problems today?"

Jesus smiled. "As I told you before, we heard this basketball program was making a big difference in its neighborhood and wanted to find out how they were doing it."

"So why did you leave after he was finished speaking," David asked? "We were going to honor those who had donated over fifty thousand dollars to the church remodeling program we just finished."

"I know," Jesus said, and he shook his head. "I also know most of those business owners donated their money just so they would get recognized and their names displayed on the church website. Free publicity. Now how many of them have donated to that basketball program?"

"I don't have any idea, but that's beside the point," David said.

"I'm afraid that is exactly the point," Jesus retorted. "Your church would have gotten along just fine without any of this technology or glitzy advertising. What it really needs is more programs that help those in your community who have issues."

"But we have to keep our audience engaged," David protested. "If we don't keep on the cutting edge, they will tune us out and we will lose their donations for our programs."

"The best way to keep people engaged is to positively affect those who need it the most," Jesus said.

That discussion went on awhile, but somehow the leader's answers always made more sense than the arguments made by the chair. Giving up in frustration (and remembering all the important stuff he should be doing) the chair had them escorted out of the complex and banned from the church.

As they left the building, they met the outreach leader coming out. He was rather disgruntled at how little attention the congregation had paid to his message, and how he had been prevented from talking to the donors even though he was asking for a far more modest amount than any of them had donated to the sanctuary remodel effort. Much to the dismay of the ushers carefully guarding the building, they ended up walking together to the nearby Bread Crumbs Cafe and had a long discussion about what defines a true outreach ministry.

Reflections

Mark 7:6-7 He replied, "Isaiah was right when he prophesied about you hypocrites, as it is written; "These people honor me with their lips, but their hearts are far from me. They worship me in vain; their teachings are mere human rules.""

This story plays on the cliche about large churches-the only way they get so many members is by focusing on entertaining them or filling them with platitudes to excuse their living instead of confronting them about their sins. While this is unfortunately true about some large churches, it can also be said about many small and medium sized churches as well. I am happy to affirm North Point Church does not reflect the attitudes reflected in this story after meeting one of its pastors and a few members at a Souly Business retreat.

The size of a church isn't determined by how well they entertain their congregation. It is based more on how welcoming they are to visitors, the quality of content and how comfortable someone feels while they are there. This has more to do with the attitudes of the people who go there and their leadership than anything else. It also has a lot to do with how willing the church is to adopt the culture of the people in the area, hopefully without compromising the true message of Christ in the process.

A growing church will have at least some of the characteristics listed here. They adopt the local culture-Cowboy Church with western music around ranches, contemporary music and lots of technology near college campuses and white-collar areas, etc. They make sure you are greeted sincerely by at least two people before you sit down, and the greeters know the answer to typical questions such as where the restrooms are and children's ministry details. There is a manned area where they can find out more detailed information about the church. Typically there is someplace they can get something to drink. The message is delivered in a language they use and understand, and there are people available to answer questions about it afterwards. There are small groups for people to get involved in that address issues they are facing as well.

A stagnant or dying church has the opposite characteristics. A visitor is ignored or, even worse, stared at when they come in and nobody greets them, except maybe the pastor. There isn't a welcome center, and they have to chase someone down to find out what to do with their kids. They stick out like a sore thumb because they didn't know there was a dress code. The message is changed to address them in some way and is full of religious words they don't have a clue what they mean. When the service is over people either rush out the door before you can talk to them or run to their cliques and ignore the newcomers.

There is one distinct advantage larger churches have to address these issues: the more people who attend makes it easier to fill volunteer positions such as Sunday School/Children's Church teachers, ushers and small group leaders. The 80/20 rule generally still applies in that 20% of the attendees do the work while 80% just show up, but the larger numbers means Aunt Betty isn't always cranky because she is trying to run the Sunday School, play the piano and teach the Children's Church lesson every Sunday she shows up. Trying to keep volunteer positions filled is a struggle for all churches, and it would be wiser for churches to drop programs nobody willingly fills and are no longer relevant to their congregation.

Questions for Contemplation

1. Do you consistently attend a church? Why or why not?

2. Does the church you attend fit the growing or dying model?

3. Which part of the 80/20 rule do you fill? What role do you play in reinforcing the growing or dying model of church?

4. Is your church culturally sensitive or insensitive? How does their cultural sensitivity help or hinder their ability to reach those in the community?

5. Would a visitor without any religious exposure be able to understand what the music and message is about?

Call to Action

Don't be so busy filling roles you can't meet the needs of the congregation. No matter what the size of your church is, find out what your attendees need and focus on them instead of fighting to maintain the status quo. If that means eliminating Sunday School that only a handful attend to provide Alcoholics Anonymous and drug rehab classes, do it. If it means ending midweek services and replacing them with small groups on different days to work around school and work schedules, do it. If it means replacing the red carpet you fought so hard over a couple years ago that it caused a church split, do it.

While there aren't any large groups dedicated to helping churches focus on caring for their communities, there are several church consultants available who can walk you through identifying what the needs are and effective ways to address them. They aren't cheap, but if you follow their recommendations both your church and community can benefit. Perhaps a good way to begin is for the church leaders to read the writings of former church leaders such as John, Paul, Saint Aquinas, Martin Luther and John Wesley.

It is important to remember that all the religious traditions, dress styles, music and liturgies we now hold sacred were created hundreds or thousands of years after Jesus Christ was on Earth. In fact, the Pharisees and Sadducees were favorite targets of Jesus because they focused on trying to follow all of the hundreds of rules they created and no longer cared for the people (Matthew 5:16-12, Matthew 23:13-15, Mark 7:1-23). For those of you hung up on hymns, just remember most of the hymns you sing in church didn't exist until those contemporary song writers John Wesley and Fanny Crosby wrote them. If you believe following a liturgy is the only way to go, remember most of them weren't written until Constantine came on the scene hundreds of years after Christ. For those who believe women must wear long dresses and not cut their hair, remember that dress code didn't exist until the Puritans placed a hold on fashion at the time they were established. Please feel free to let go of the externals and focus on what Jesus taught was important- loving yourself and your neighbor, and caring for those around you.

7. THE HOUSE

The south-western part of Nebraska is a farmer's dream. Originally covered with prairie grass, it was homesteaded and turned into farms. After the Dust Bowl farmers began strip farming, so swaths of wheat now burst between fallow land soaking in moisture, weaving shadows of rich soil between the bounty of harvest. As small farmers were squeezed out because of increasing costs, the farms consolidated. Now you can stop at the top of a hill and see wheat fading into the horizon, interrupted only by a dirt road every mile and an occasional stream marked by a trail of trees.

Scattered within the fields are small farming communities, anchored by a grain elevator and, if they are lucky enough to have enough kids to avoid consolidation, a school. Other mandatory buildings include a post office, at least two churches and a café for the farmers to drive into town and sip coffee while discussing weather and politics if it is too wet to work the fields. There are usually less than a couple hundred people in the town, most of whom can trace their roots in the area back several generations. Jobs outside the fields are scarce and don't pay that well, but everyone works together to build communities where patriotism and faith are more important than how much money someone has.

Furnas County sits on the border with Kansas, about halfway down the list of counties in Nebraska based on population. Beaver City is the county seat, sitting off Highway 89 next to Beaver Creek. It is small, with large lots that allows homes to have gardens and lawns with trees for kids or grandkids to explore. Everyone knows everyone else's business but is usually wise enough to be good neighbors and help out if needed and otherwise live and let live.

On the corner of 11th and M sits an old single-story house with a detached garage. It was the home of one of the original settlers, the outside covered with asbestos tiles slathered with Royal Blue paint fading and peeling off the edges. The trim is covered with white paint, spiderwebbed with age and pulling away from the dehydrated caulking which gave up its fight against the wind years ago.

Ora and Lenore Gove lived there, a fixture in the town for decades. When they bought the house, he worked at the local dairy farm, working the cows and milking machines twice a day. When it shut down because of a drought, he started delivering for the local bakery until it, too, closed its doors. After that he took care of yards, hauling their grass and leaves in his old Chevy pickup when he wasn't taking care of his own.

As battered as the outside of their house was, their yard was a thing of beauty. The back end of the house was surrounded by a flower garden, crowned with rose bushes and an ancient peony bush that covered the back end of the house with its massive showers of pink blossoms. A few feet behind the flowers was their vegetable garden which stretched back to the alley. As bountiful as the flower garden was, the vegetable garden exceeded its bounty and yielded rows of shining jars filled with enough produce to last the winter.

It had been a fairly wet summer and projections for the wheat harvest were high, so futures prices had been dropping. Beef prices were rising so farmers were putting more wheat into hay to feed their livestock over the winter than usual. The extra acres put under the swather meant local farmers were struggling to finish the work between thunderstorms and the wheat stems started losing nutritional value as they dried.

One afternoon a haying crew rolled into town, fresh off their last job around Burns, Wyoming. There were thirteen of them, which meant they took over most of the Furnas County Inn, the only hotel in town. They worked daylight to dusk in the fields, so the only entertainment available when they got back to town was walking through the streets of the small community.

A few nights later Ora was outside picking strawberries when some of the group walked by. They waved and said hi. He straightened a bit to stretch his back and asked them how the harvest was going. After a bit of banter about how many bales they were getting per acre, the number of flat tires they had in the rocky fields and the biggest rattlesnake they had ever caught in a bale, he waved them over to pick a few strawberries for themselves while they talked.

Conversation wandered around, from the garden to the weather to the house where they lived. He said it was at least eighty years old, and still pretty solid. The roof had been redone about fifteen years ago and the water heater had been replaced, but the wall furnaces they used for heat kept them comfortable. When the light faded and the fireflies began winking in the grass, one of the men brought up the color of the house.

"There has to be a story behind the color of the house," Jesus said. "What can you tell me about it?"

"That is Royal Blue," Ora replied. "Lenore picked it out the year we moved in. It took us longer to paint the house than it did for us to unpack the few things we had back then."

"If you had the chance to do it over again, would you paint it the same color or use a different one?" Jesus asked.

Ora laughed. "Oh, we've talked about that a lot over the years. One thing about it, our house is easy to find. We think a light green might have been a better choice, though."

"Light green. Anything specific?" Jesus asked.

"Well, I think her favorite color is Seafoam these days," said Ora.

By that time daylight had given up, and the fireflies danced along the tops of the roses. Ora told the crew good night and headed inside with his harvest. The crew walked back to their hotel rooms, the dark brown dust on their clothes spotted with red juice from the fresh strawberries they had just eaten.

That night it rained cats and dogs, with a few stray rabbits thrown in for good measure. When the crew woke up the next morning the ground was soaked, and it would take a couple days for it to dry out enough to finish haying. With a couple days off Jesus and Judas drove over to the Ag Valley Co-op in Norton, Kansas. An hour later they headed back with a load of caulking, Seafoam and white exterior paint and a collection of utility knives and paint brushes.

When they got back, they rounded up the rest of the crew as they finished their breakfast sandwiches from the gas station next door to the hotel and headed over to Ora and Lenore's house. As the crew started scraping and sanding the paint, Jesus drove over to the high school and convinced the boys playing basketball in the playground to join in the effort. They made a quick stop at Kelly's Super Mart for coffee, pop and pizzas, then headed back to join in the fun.

When they reached the house most of the windows had been prepped. John and Andrew were caulking the cracks along the windowpanes that let in the drafts. Within a couple hours the gaps were filled and loose paint removed, so the group started priming the walls while the caulking set up.

The percolator in the kitchen put out a steady supply of coffee. The first round of pizzas came out of the oven when the noon whistle blew. By the time the food was gone the caulking had set up enough to paint over, so those with the steadiest hands started trimming where the first coat of green was drying.

The day was hot and steamy, but the paint soaked in and dried quickly. The house was relatively small and there was plenty of help, so the work moved quickly. Bartholomew and Philip spent part of the afternoon trimming the flowers far enough away from the back wall so it could be painted, with plenty of supervision from Ora. By the time darkness fell all the cracks were filled and the tiles covered with primer. The kids headed home for supper while the crew cleaned the brushes and cleaned up, then everyone turned in for the night.

The next day the crew headed back to finish the job. Several of the boys came back as well. Fueled by coffee and pop they finished the last coat of paint before lunch. Lenore's cousin Blanche who lived behind them came over with her famous sloppy joes for lunch which complemented the home-made rolls she had baked yesterday. Full of satisfaction at a job well done, and their stomachs loaded with deliciousness, the crew headed back to the hotel for an afternoon of rest before returning to the fields the next day.

The haying crew rolled out of town a couple days later, but they had changed the town while they were there. They brought the town closer together, and the faded blue house at the edge of town was now a beautiful green with bright white trim. Ora and Lenore enjoyed the color, and the house was easier to keep warm with the wind in check. The whole town seemed a little brighter after that, and the shiny green house on the corner made even the coldest winter day a little warmer.

Reflections

Proverbs 29:7 The righteous care about justice for the poor, but the wicked have no such concern.

Anywhere you go you can find houses in disrepair. Some just need repainted, while others have holes in the roof or wall that need repaired. While some of these houses are owned by slum lords, many of them are owned by Senior Citizens or people with handicaps with minimal income who are unable to perform routine maintenance on their own homes.

Some cities have laws that fine people who do not cut their grass, have trash in their yards or do not clean their sidewalks. This can be an ongoing problem for those who can't afford to pay someone to do the work for them. This is especially a problem when their owners end up in the hospital or have to move into rehab or long-term care centers due to health issues.

Questions for Contemplation

1. Do you know anyone in your community with deferred maintenance issues who are unable to take care of it themselves?

2. Are there any organizations in your area who focus on either weatherizing or performing deferred maintenance for those in need?

3. Some communities coordinate with all of their volunteer organizations to help clean up the community. This frequently is done on Martin Luther King Day, but not always. Who organizes these efforts in your area? If your community does not do this, what steps could your church take to organize one?

4. Many church youth and Bible study groups help a local family or individual on their own at least once a year. What would it take for a group you are a part of to change the life of at least one homeowner this year?

5. Everyone has busy schedules and their own homes to take care of. They are also concerned about their property value, which is affected by the condition of other houses in the neighborhood. How would helping out your struggling neighbors either through organized efforts or volunteering your own time affect the real estate values and morale of the area you live in?

Call to Action

As with most of the issues mentioned in this book, volunteers and the financial resources to pay for supplies are the biggest needs to help bring houses back to good condition. In this case, someone with the knowledge and equipment is extremely important to fix roofing and other major repair issues. Organization is also key to recruit enough people to take care of an issue in a day. If you are able to fill any of these roles you can play a valuable role in improving your community and improving the morale of those who are unable to take care of these issues themselves.

There are some organizations which focus on helping winterize and repair homes for those who can't do it themselves. One is the Home Repair Relief Project. Another is the Handyman Ministries, who is looking for other churches to join their crusade. Of One Accord is repair ministry based in the Appalachia area. To connect with an organization in your area check with your local church for more information.

8. THE JALOPY

It started as a typical summer morning in Alma, Kansas. The heat was just starting to settle onto the streets of the small town of eight hundred. A mother and her two toddlers coaxed the screech out of the swing set in the park. Behind them eight teens played baseball on the town field, rotating positions after each out. Across the railroad tracks an old man sat on a bench outside of the Stop and Shop, sipping coffee as he waited for the eleven forty-five freight to go by. An occasional pickup drove up Highway 99 to the Co-op, but other than that the streets were quiet.

Two things happened that prevented the day from joining the long list of excruciatingly ordinary days there. They would have been fodder for gossip by themselves, with a good chance of making the front page of the Wabaunsee County Signal-Enterprise. The way they came together made it a day remembered for decades.

Just after eleven a stranger walked into town. Somewhere in his thirties, he was the classic hippie. His rugged olive face was framed with dark brown hair that fell to his waist. A long, stained leather coat flapped around his patched jeans and faded t-shirt. A military backpack with his belongings hung from his shoulders. He went into the store, made small talk with the owners as he bought food for a simple lunch, then joined the old man on the bench. They swapped stories and watched the kids play in the park, waiting for someone to stop that might take him farther on his way as he ate.

At eleven thirty-eight a dot appeared south of town on the highway, noticeable because of how slowly it was moving. It turned out to be a rusty 1990 Ford Fairmont station wagon, chased by a cloud of blue smoke. The motor was erratic, frequently sputtering and pounding away with an ominous knock, but still going. It made you want to ask two questions: first, how it kept going; and second, who would be crazy enough to take it on a trip.

The highway has a dip, then a moderate grade building up to the tracks on the south side. As the car hit the dip something shook loose, and the motor sputtered to a stop. The wagon coasted up the rise and creaked to a stop sitting across the tracks. The man driving the car tried to coax the motor to life once again, but it refused.

Just as the car stopped, the freight began sounding its horn on its way into town. The engineer blew his horn several times, then clicked on the emergency brake when the car in its way didn't move. Metal screeched, sparks flew and the train began to slow, but it was obvious it would never stop in time.

The mother pushing her kids on the swing froze, a look of horror on her face. The kids playing baseball closest to the highway took off running towards the car to push it off the tracks, but there wasn't any way they could reach it in time. The old man pulled himself off the bench with his cane and leaned forward, trying to will the collision from happening. The hippie finished throwing his trash away and watched intently. Only five seconds had passed, but the train had closed to within five hundred yards of the stranded car.

A man and women in their thirties jumped out of the car and began trying to pull two young kids out of car seats in the back. They frantically pulled on the straps of the old, worn seats, but the buckles and latches stubbornly refused to budge. Refusing to think of their own peril they struggled on, ignoring the train now a scant two hundred yards from the passenger door.

"Train be still! Car be healed." The words came from the hippie, suddenly a figure of power. He held out one hand towards each vehicle as he uttered the words, palms open. Everyone heard the sound over the screaming and screeching, but only the old man saw who spoke them.

The train shuddered, then froze in place fifty feet from the stranded family in the car. Later the engineer said it was as if it had been hit by a gigantic hammer. And it was over. No more movement, no more noise, the train engine just sat there purring softly like a kitten.

The mother grabbed her kids off the swing and headed towards the car to make sure everyone was ok. The teens rushed over to push the car off the tracks. The old man leaned against his cane, panting, than sat down heavily. He turned to ask the hippie what had happened, but he was gone. As the old man looked down the street, he saw him getting into a car headed north with his backpack.

The family in the car was scared, of course, but they were all fine. After a few minutes of mass confusion and everyone asking if they were ok, they turned to the business of getting the car off the tracks. The father got in to steer, then hit the ignition out of habit. The engine roared to life, running like it was brand new and he drove the car to a parking space by the store. Everyone went inside to recover and talk about what happened.

It turned out the stranded family was a young preacher, just out of seminary, headed towards his first pastorate in Nebraska City, Nebraska. Everything they owned was in the wagon, and money was in short supply. This trip, and to a big extent the job ahead of them, was a step of faith.

As their story unfolded, so did the food. They were ushered to a table and pizza was rushed over, along with milk for the baby. Word circulated fast in the small town, and donations flew in to help them finish their journey and get settled in their new life. A mechanic came over from the local garage, but the car engine now ran flawlessly. The crowd continued to grow, and their story was repeated around town.

The big topic of discussion was about what had actually happened. Some said they heard words. Others insisted it was thunder, even though the sky was clear. The old man eased off the bench, went inside, and shared what he had seen-the hippie stand up and say some words, and that's when the train stopped. They wished they could talk to him and find out who he was, but he was gone. He was gone, but the legacy he left grew.

When the family couldn't possibly eat or drink anything more, they went out to the car to continue their journey. Their old car seats had disappeared and new ones sat in their place. The pastor from the United Methodist Church gave them the donations that had been gathered, which was more than enough to get them through their first month. As the final thank you and good luck was exchanged, the preacher fired up the car and purred north once again for the final one hundred fifty miles of the trip. The freight train headed out as well, after undergoing a security check. Alma turned back to its business, but never to what was normal before.

Reflections

Luke 14:5 Then he asked them, "If one of you has a child or an ox that falls into a well on the Sabbath day, will you not immediately pull it out?"

Alma, Kansas is a "sleepy" farm town sitting about halfway between the two state universities. It has a booming antiques business, but its main claim to fame is a small dairy that produces amazing cheeses carried by several local stores. There are two ways to cross the railroad into town: one is the crossing here, and for the adventurous there is a single-lane wooden overpass without any side rails.

Vehicles with mechanical issues will be with us until they perfect transporters. This isn't just an issue with older cars, but usually they are more susceptible to having issues. The condition of a car has more to do with how well it has been maintained than its age, once the initial kinks are worked out. Since having a car to get around in is a necessity in smaller cities and rural areas, it is something we all need to deal with at some point.

Questions for Contemplation

1. Part of being financially responsible is keeping "stuff" longer and taking care of it instead of throwing things away and buying new ones. I will watch my second car that I bought used roll over 200,000 miles soon, barring something drastic. While paying for maintenance can be pricey, it is not as expensive as having a large monthly car payment on top of taxes and insurance. Is the vehicle(s) you drive based on being financially responsible or keeping up appearances? How has this affected other aspects of your life?

2. Having an engine or transmission repair that costs $1,500.00 or more seems expensive, but in reality it is the equivalent of paying a $350.00 car payment for just over four months. Does this change your perspective on how driving an older car that is paid for should be a financial decision instead of one based on culture and materialism?

3. The key to taking materialism out of the things we buy is to understand they are just tools to use in fulfilling God's mission. A car is a tool to get you and your family to where they need to be. It is also a tool to care for those in need by taking them to the store or doctor's appointments or to church. Considering what you have done in your vehicle in the last month, how has it fulfilled God's calling to care for your family and your community?

4. Some people are like McGyver and can fix anything with a toothpick and duct tape. Others are like me who have to have a manual or YouTube video of how to change spark plugs and it still takes an hour to do it. Do you have the skills to help someone repair their vehicle, or are you better suited to paying someone else do the work? How does your skill set affect your interest in helping others with their vehicle repairs?

5. The longer you put off repairing something the more expensive it becomes. For example, if you replace the brake pads when they first start squealing it will relatively inexpensive, but ignoring it will make the repair cost two or three times as much because you will have to replace the rotors as well. Even though it is a financial stretch to make repairs, have you ever considered the high cost of waiting while the problem gets worse? Can you think of a time when putting off asking forgiveness for a sin made the problem worse?

Call to Action

If you drive a car, you should expect to have expenses to take care of it. This starts with license and insurance, but also oil changes and tune-ups. In West Virginia this includes new tires and brakes about once a year as well, but these last much longer in Kansas and Wyoming. The point of maintenance is a fact of life and should be expected. That is why everyone should set aside money every month in an emergency fund. While car maintenance is expected and not technically an emergency, having money set aside you can access easily is a key to avoiding additional debt.

Most car maintenance can be done at home by someone who knows what they are doing. This is the least expensive way to do it, since it avoids paying for a mechanic and related shop fees. If you are mechanically declined like I am, then paying someone else to perform the work pays for itself in saved time and the knowledge it was done correctly.

There are groups who perform maintenance for those who can't afford it. As I'm writing this an article came up on Facebook for God's Garage, sponsored by Crossroads Church in Kokomo, Indiana. His Hands Auto helps repair vehicles and also helps connect people who need cars with vehicles. The Car Ministry in Falls Church, Virginia is focused on connecting people with cars but not on repairing them. Some churches do this as a ministry monthly or quarterly as well. Contact your local church or Christian assistance organization to see if there are any car ministries in your area.

9. THE CONFERENCE

George Ellis had had enough. After three days of didactic debate, the delegate from Grand Island waved his hand at the chairman.

"The Chair recognizes Mr. Ellis," Bishop McFerson intoned.

"We have gone over this point for an hour, and I think everyone has beaten their horse to death. I move the previous question," George stated.

There was a sigh of relief from the delegates sitting on cramped pews in the sweltering tabernacle on the district campground. Several observers had slipped into the mix as rumors spread the debate was almost over.

The assembly was varied and eclectic. Bishop McFerson sat at a table on the platform where the pulpit usually stood, still a commanding figure at seventy two. His grey hair suggested an attempt at a comb-over, but was too short to accomplish anything more than random tufts thrusting defiantly thorough a glaze of Vitalis. His dark blue suit threatened to swallow him, especially when he slouched in his seat. His voice was crisp and authoritative, at times threatening the stodgy grey microphone sitting in front of him, more out of tradition than need.

At his right sat the vice chair, Reverend Jim Thorton. He was remarkable only in how average he was-about five foot seven, somewhere in his fifties with salt and pepper hair and a face that looked like the generic form one would start with when sketching a suspect. He wore a simple black suit with just the hint of pinstripes, sleeves a little short and pants a little long, with a burgundy tie that stirred up some controversy among the assembly. Even when there was absolutely nothing to do during the long debates he would pick up a random sheet of paper from the stacks in front of him, scribble a note on it and pass it to the bishop, who would peer anxiously at it and nod before looking back to the speaker.

The left side of the table was occupied by the vice-chair Right Reverend Larry Burns, a tour de force. Taller than most men, he took up the space of three. Nobody was quite sure what the distinction was that made him a Right Reverend, but any challenge to his title caused the questioner to regret his indiscretion. A fashionable grey suit tried to contain him, and an oversize matching grey tie struggled to reach halfway down his stomach. He had been a major contributor to this debate, which was typical, and had introduced the topic in the first place-but only after several delegates had threatened to revolt if it wasn't raised. His booming voice frequently overpowered the small sound system, an edge he took advantage of when things weren't going the direction he felt was appropriate.

The delegates were a mix of preachers and elders from the denomination. Despite the fact they came from a wide range of backgrounds and occupations, all were dressed in dark suits with unassuming ties. Their haircuts ranged from very conservative to military to bald. Overall their attitude was tense, tired and frustrated, since every effort to make changes had been stonewalled and viewed with suspicion. They overwhelmingly approved the motion to vote on the original question, convinced any more efforts to change would just die in a tirade of disapproval and call into question their suitability to lead a church.

The observers were an interesting mix as well. Most were wives of the delegates, all wearing simple dresses with long sleeves and hems at least two inches below their knees. The dresses were mostly homemade, since the accepted style hadn't been sold in stores for over a hundred years. Some creativity showed through with different lace patterns or mixing colors, but the overall look was somber. Their sighs and exchanged looks showed a healthy degree of communication within the building, and a great deal more once they escaped the confines of the meeting.

A few children were scattered among the mothers. All the girls wore simple dresses, and the boys wore dress pants and long sleeves. They had been trained to sit silently during the meetings, although occasional fidgets manifested involuntarily. Here and there one could find some dirt or grass stains on their clothes from clandestine games played before being snatched from their frivolity to sit with a parent to make sure they stayed out of trouble and maintained the proper attitude of worship and meditation.

There was a group that stood out from the rest, however. The group of thirteen had wandered into the meeting apparently at random, and the leader sat in the back pew with a mix of followers that changed randomly. They wore faded jeans and an odd assortment of shirts, ranging from old event shirts to polos to the leader and his collection of Hawaiian shirts. Several of the attendees had offered to loan them more appropriate clothing for the event, but they had declined which created a bit of an uproar. However, as long as they stayed quiet and kept their long hair up in ponytails, nobody could come up with a believable excuse to exclude them from the events. Besides, they were friendly and kept everyone entertained with quaint stories that seemed to answer their questions better than the long, droning sermons fired during the evening services.

"All in favor of the modifications to the Code of Conduct in the discipline please say "Aye," Bishop McPherson stated. Three of the younger pastors said "Aye," which immediately drew a storm of raised eyebrows and calculating looks in their direction. "All opposed say nay." There was a loud chorus in response

"The modifications have been rejected for consideration by the General Conference next year. This being the last matter of business before the Conference, I declare the fifty-first District Conference adjourned." With that Bishop McFerson tucked

his gavel into the inner pocket of his suit jacket, stretched slowly, then left the platform. Reverend Thorton slowly stacked his papers for filing and future compilation into detailed minutes, carefully sorting them into separate compartments in his briefcase. The Right Reverend Burns made a beeline for the preachers who dared to express dissatisfaction with the group-think he had forced on the delegates.

Just as the Right Reverend had puffed his way up to speed on his way past the first row of pews, he bounced off the Hawaiian shirt clad leader of the misfits. How the hippie had managed to make it to the front of the room in the time the Right Reverend Burns took to get off the platform gave him pause, but it didn't stop his huff of annoyance at his mission being disrupted. The leader, who called himself Jesus, put his hand on the Right Reverend's shoulder, which somehow froze him in place. Jesus then walked a couple more steps to the front of the room and began speaking in a voice which carried over the noise and quieted the room immediately.

"You've been wondering why we came here. We wanted to witness this historic event for ourselves. You're probably thinking that nothing historic happened here today, and you're right. You had the first chance in several years to turn your church into a vibrant, growing organization following God's mission. Instead you voted to maintain the status quo."

Gasps were heard from several members. The Right Reverend Burns tried with all his might to launch into a rambling invective condemning this stranger and his impertinent outburst, but realized his tongue was frozen as well as his feet. The dissenting pastors nodded their agreement, and the room became silent as Jesus continued.

"Your churches are empty. Your revivals and outreach efforts fall flat. The only way your pastors survive is to work full-time. Most of the people in this room think that is because of persecution brought on by your righteous lives. In reality it is self-imposed ostracism because of your religion."

"You show your religion in your dress. Your discipline

says women must wear long hair and dresses, and men must wear short hair, pants and long sleeves. You have faithfully maintained the traditions of the Puritans. However, if you dressed as Jesus dressed you would all be wearing robes. If you wore the original dress code, you would be wearing animal skins. Paul does give guidelines for women to have long hair and men short hair and dress modestly, but what you have turned it into is pharisaical laws."

"You ban everyone from drinking alcohol. This cracks me up the most, since my first miracle was turning water into wine- and yes, I did drink it. Paul specifically touts the health benefits of drinking wine to Timothy. Drinking wine was a part of Jewish culture and remains so to this day. The Bible does caution against excess in several places, but the only place abstaining mentioned in the Old Testament is when people take religious oaths. Since I don't see anyone eating vegetarian diets and men letting your hair grow, I know none of you have taken those oaths, so either go all the way and do those as well or drop the religious pretense of this lifestyle choice."

"I don't understand your dreadfully formal ritual celebrating Communion. When I instituted the practice, and the way the early church celebrated it, was an informal remembrance at the end of a weekly common meal. In other words, this was an affirmation of a common belief, not a terribly stuffy ritual dreaded by the participants. It should be a positive family experience, not a dreaded religious ritual."

"The whole section on personal behavior most of you just voted to keep in the discipline should be called the fear section, because all of it is based on the fear of doing something that might lead to doing something that might cause you to sin. Don't drink alcohol, because it might lead to getting drunk. Don't dress like everyone else, because you might end up wearing something that isn't modest. Don't accumulate wealth, because it might lead to money being an idol for you. Don't use the internet because it might lead you to look at porn. Don't go to movies because you might not be able to read the promotions to find out if it is appropriate or not. The list goes on and on."

"The list of rules you have fits perfectly with the list of rules the Pharisees came up with-and it keeps growing like theirs did. They had a dress code. Their behavior code was much more complex, but the basics are the same. What you have created is a very strict religion, and anyone that doesn't follow your religion is considered an outcast."

"God has no interest in another religion. There are plenty of them running around, and they are all designed to keep people failing so they are stuck in fear and misery. God didn't send me to die on the cross to bring more misery, but to establish a relationship of freedom. When pressed to build a religion I responded by compressing the Ten Commandments into two: love God with your heart, soul and mind, and love your neighbors as yourself."

"Most of you can't love your neighbors, because you don't love yourselves. You deny your status as sons and daughters of God, and by doing this you deny those privileges to the people you interact with. Like the Pharisees you loathe yourselves because you fail to keep all the religious rules you've created for yourselves, and you look at your neighbors with even more loathing because they don't try to keep your rules."

"How many of you have a list of rules your friends have to keep, or they are instantly cut off from any contact with you? Yet that is how you insist God treats you. A healthy relationship has the understanding that you will fail each other, sometimes repeatedly in certain areas, but those errors are met with forgiveness and working through issues together to develop a deeper relationship. That is how God wants to have a relationship with you."

"What you have accomplished here today was a monumental religious triumph, but a complete failure as Christians. Now that the vote is over, I hope you stop blustering and take some time to seriously examine your positions from a scriptural, not religious, standpoint. Stop the rationalizations and go back to being scriptural. If you truly do that, the results will be much different the next time you discuss this."

"We will be leaving now. I'm sure some of you have questions for us, and some of you just want to argue to prove yourself right, but all the answers are in your Bible. It was enlightening sitting here listening to the doctors argue, but it is time to for us to find those who know they are sick and take care of them. Please consider after we're gone how effective you are at being doctors if you don't really understand either the disease or the treatment for it."

After Jesus was done talking, he and his disciples walked out to their minivan. Some of the crowd followed them outside to say their farewells, but most remained where they were in a dazed silence. The van started in a cloud of smoke and eased out onto the road. Their exit brought relief to several of the regulars, and for the most part left the proceedings unchanged other than planting seeds in the minds of a few who were really listening.

Reflections

Matthew 23:23 "Woe to you, teachers of the law and Pharisees, you hypocrites! You give a tenth of your spices—mint, dill and cumin. But you have neglected the more important matters of the law—justice, mercy and faithfulness. You should have practiced the latter, without neglecting the former.

A common question of unbelievers is why there are so many different churches. The answer is simple: like any family, Christians have fights. If the fight is between one or two Christians, they either start attending a different church or just stop going. If it is several people on each side in a church fighting, one group of them might leave and start their own church. If there are many people in more than one church in a denomination fighting, they all might leave and start their denomination. This typically happens for two reasons: if the issue is important enough, or if the personalities involved are strong. I would be hypocritical to pretend this only happens with churches, since the same thing happens with all of society from marriages to social clubs on to businesses and governments.

There are three types of issues people fight about in churches. The first issue is doctrine, or what the church believes and teaches about the Bible. The second issue is tradition, or the way the church teaches to do things that either aren't mentioned or have more than one side mentioned in the Bible. The third issue is simply preferences, or personal likes and dislikes. While all of these are important in your personal walk with God, doctrine is the only one based on clearly defined scripture and may be important enough to attend a different church over.

Doctrine can be divided into three areas. The first type of doctrine is "blood" or theological foundations such as the way of salvation, the Trinity and the virgin birth. The second type of doctrine is "ink" which can be traced back through the Bible but may be reasonably interpreted more than one way such as the role of baptism, eternal security and predestination. The last type of doctrine is written in "pencil" and mainly includes behaviors such as drinking alcohol and how homosexuality is treated.

Alcohol is a hot topic that falls in the pencil doctrines of a church. I have not been able to find any Biblical commentaries claiming alcoholic wine did not exist before the 1700's. If you have questions about the alcoholic content of wine in the Bible you would be better off having a long conversation with a rabbi than modern day commentators. In the meantime, the blog by Joe Thorn at http://www.doctrineanddevotion.com/blog/wine would be a good read on the topic .

Traditions play a big role in many denominational splits. While some may include traditions under pencil doctrines, this is a misperception since you cannot find scriptural references for them. Traditions include such diverse topics as liturgies, singing and preaching styles, dress codes and entertainment choices (gambling, watching TV and movies, amusement parks, etc.)

Preferences are personal likes and dislikes, and they play a role in many church splits. The favorite example is fights over new carpet or paint colors. Other popular examples are retaining pastors, building or remodeling projects and how to handle scandals.

Questions for Contemplation

1. It is typical for churches to have disagreements occasionally. What was the last issue your church faced? Does it qualify as doctrine, tradition or preference?

2. Churches that have existed for at least ten years tend to have one area where most disagreements come from. What is the most frequent area of disagreement in your church?

3. If you have experienced a church or denominational split, what were the main factors behind it?

4. Do your local church leaders focus more on doctrinal

issues than traditions and preferences? How does their focus affect its ability to reach out to and care for your local community?

5. Consider the reasons you attend your current church and how effective it is in performing the mission of the Great Commission. How would the members and community be rewarded if it would stop fighting over pencil doctrines, traditions and preferences with other churches and combine your efforts?

Call to Action

The first step towards overcoming legalistic or antagonistic confrontations in a church, or even a community, is to examine your beliefs and break them down into what is doctrinal or if they are just what you are used to. Once you have sorted the important things from the other distractions, you may need to re-evaluate your priorities and if things you have fought over in the past actually contribute to God's mission.

The next step is to demonstrate any new priorities to your church (and community). If you have been actively contributing to disagreements or confrontations about minor issues, apologize for your role and be the negotiator or peacemaker in the situation. You can never underestimate the change one person can create when they refocus on what is important.

10. FAKE PATTY'S DAY

Three tables were shoved together in the middle of Bluestem Bistro the first Saturday of March. Thirteen men crowded around them, some chairs shoved in awkward positions to leave room for people to squeeze by on either side. They looked like graduate students outfitted in hoodies and jeans or khakis, huddled up to plan their next project. Cups of coffee in various flavors and colors teetered precariously in the middle of the table, crammed between dishes with scraps of biscuits and gravy and freshly baked scones. Conversation was difficult due to the crowded room, but you could make out bits of voices as they bounced off the original artwork exhibited on the walls.

"... sure in the right town?"

"... quiet as a seminary before finals."

"A few cones in the road doesn't mean...."

The bell above the door jingled as a stream of new customers walked in. Some of the disciples glanced up at the new arrivals, but their appearances earned them a longer look. Several of the group wore cheap green t-shirts with "Fake Patty's Day" printed on them. Green was a common color, as was a general odor of alcohol even though it was only ten in the morning. One of the men wobbled slightly as he stood at the counter to order. Their conversation was boisterous and centered on their planned drinking activities for the day, and how this round of coffee would help stave off getting blitzed for a little while.

The loud and constant talk from the newcomers made conversation impossible. When their last coffees slid across the counter, they jostled their way out the door. The ensuing quiet was almost eerie. The plates of the men at the table were emptied, and there was a rush to the counter for refills after it cleared out. With full stomachs and new doses of caffeine on the way, the tone of their conversation changed.

"Well, now I understand why we're here better," Peter said. Even though he was used to the rough and tumble life of the outcast, this early display of debauchery was a bit more than The Rock was used to.

The number of people in the street outside the front window increased as the bright sun woke more of the revelers. Business in the Aggieville bars was at full throttle and lines began to form outside of a few. A tall, thin blonde man walked up to the line waiting to get into the Bomb Bar across the street. After a few seconds he took a roundabout swing at the burly man with a beard standing in front of him and the fight was on. Two of the others in line pulled them apart and made the aggressor move on down the street, where he disappeared before the police arrived. There were frequent bouts of pushing and shoving as people staggering down the street bumped into each other.

"Time to go out there," Jesus said.

The group picked up their empty plates and carried them to the dirty dish tray on top of the trash bin. As the stack of dirty dishes reached the top of the bin a new rush of partyers walked in, looking for a jolt of sobriety in between bars full of green beer and drunken college students trying to hook up with the influx of visitors in town. They squeezed through the crowd between the counter and door, exiting the street as the first round of bands at the bars began their sound checks.

They turned right, heading towards the heavier concentration of bars in the short section of party town, Kansas style. On the opposite side of the street a policewoman bent over a girl vomiting as she lay on the curb while her partner called for an ambulance as the first case of alcohol poisoning began its trip through the EMS system. Most people just walked by, but one man with an eye swollen shut from a recent fight leaned against the wall watching the action.

A few doors down an older man with a straggling beard

leaned against the doorway of the closed hair salon. His head bobbed up and down as he struggled to maintain consciousness as the alcoholic fog smothered his brain. His hands twitched in rhythm with the mental contortions of years of drug abuse ravaging his body.

A policeman on the far end of the block smiled and greeted an older gentleman walking down the street pushing a bicycle. Garbage bags swung from both handlebars, their sides threatening to burst as he picked up an unending supply of aluminum cans scattered on the sidewalks and streets. He ambled along until he reached the bistro the group had just left, where he headed in for his usual morning coffee and snack. With any luck someone he knew would be there willing to play a few games of Uno before he decided to continue his mission of cleaning up the street before it became too crowded.

Jesus and his disciples walked the few blocks of businesses crowded between blocks of student apartments several times that morning. They would greet random people and try to engage them in conversations about their spiritual life. Some would look embarrassed and quickly walk away. Some would laugh in their face and stagger through the group. A few were too drunk or high to form complete sentences and slurred a brief response. Several who were half unconscious, sitting beside buildings or on the curb, would be forced to at least start a conversation, at least until their anger or urgency for another drink goaded them enough to lurch up and walk off. A few people had meaningful conversations and asked for prayer before going off in a different direction than they had originally intended, but those conversations were few and far between.

After a few hours of literally and figuratively going in circles, the disciple's stomachs announced it was time for lunch. Since they were on the west end of the street, they headed into Chipotle for some burritos to feed their blue-collar appetites. The line of customers wound out the door, but the workers were efficient, and it didn't take long to get their food. They grabbed two tables next to each other that miraculously opened up and settled in to eat their food.

The line wound past the tables towards the counter. Some of the customers were in their usual Saturday outfits, and sported a confused look as they tried to figure out why there were so many people in the area that day. There were many versions of green t-shirts around, some from many years ago when the participant made their first Fake Patty's Day appearance. The girls generally wore short shorts or mini skirts, despite the chill in the late winter air. A few people were dressed up in green suits or party dresses, many of which were still running on the fumes of staying up all night drinking. Expressions ranged from stony silence to suppressed rage to vapid babbling. Frequently the noisiest ones were next to those who were silent and looked like they were searching for something to shut out a night of bad memories.

Jesus' attention focused on one girl as she walked up outside the window. She was an attractive (temporary) blonde dressed in a frilly silk dress. She talked incessantly, reeling from side to side as her three sorority sisters steered her in the desired direction. Her voice carried through the glass, over the noise of the din inside, until her friends shushed her.

Her dress had seen better days. Evidence of spilled drinks could be seen in several places. Her left shoulder was partially torn, either from falling down or it being pulled off roughly, at some point last night. The ruffles on the bottom of the skirt turned up where she had sat for a long period of time with them folded up under her leg. The back had dirty spots where she had leaned against outside walls that hadn't been cleaned for some time.

Her mute button fell off as they came through the door and she began to warm up as the line flowed forward. Her monologue began with how cold it was, and that she couldn't remember where she left her coat. When she stopped shivering, it transitioned to where all they had been last night, even though she couldn't remember most of it and her friends had to keep filling in the blanks. There were frequent questions about the time in concern for meeting up with someone she met last night, even though it was hours away and she wore a watch on her wrist. After a few questions about the time, her topic moved to the guy she met-even though her friends had to tell her his name and remind her what he looked like.

Jesus reached out and grabbed her arm as she came within reach. This caused all sorts of consternation among her friends, but she didn't even notice until she started to move forward with the line again and found herself detained.

"Daughter, this is not who you are," Jesus said.

"What? I'm not your daughter. I don't know who you are, you dirty old man" she responded.

"You know who I am. Listen to your heart," he said.

"My Dad was an alcoholic who abused me, and you don't look anything like him," she yelled back so loud the entire restaurant could hear. Well, at least she was the center of attention again, which she worked very hard to maintain.

"I know," Jesus replied. "I didn't ask who your earthly father was. I know who you are, and this is not it. What are you doing?"

"What does it look like I'm doing?" she asked. "I'm out partying with my friends, and when I take my new boyfriend to meet my Dad, he is going to regret what he did to me, because he's a cop!"

"I'm glad your life is going so well," he said. "Drowning your memories in alcohol never lasts very long, and your new boyfriend can't remember your name, either. Sounds like a perfect match to me. By the way, where are your friends?"

She quickly glanced behind her, discovering her friends left when she ignored their attempts to move her down the line and continued to talk to the fuzzy-headed stranger. She looked around the room and saw her friends ordering food at the counter.

"They will come back for me," she retorted. "They always do. Who do you think I am, if you know so much?"

"Do you remember when your Dad came into your room

and you cried out for help, how you always said someone came to sit by you and scared him away? That was one of my angels. You were one of my special children back then, and you still are," he said.

"The only thing special about me now is how much I can drink and how many men I can get to buy me stuff," she retorted.

"And what does all that stuff mean to you," he asked? "Is it worth trading your soul for some jewelry and temporary relief from pain?"

"No," she sobbed. "This is not the life I wanted, but I don't deserve any better. I'm not worth anything, except some easy entertainment, after what my Dad did to me."

"I died for you," he said. "Does that tell you how valuable you are to me? Let me show you how valuable you are, and what your future will be."

Jesus reached out and placed his hands over her eyes. He bowed his head and prayed briefly in Hebrew. She gasped and inhaled deeply, then relaxed. The drunken confusion clouding her eyes faded, and a peace she hadn't felt since she was very young, replaced it. He removed his hands from her head, and she stood calmly in front of him.

"Now go back to your Campus Ventures group and tell them your story," he said. "They will help you find your way from here."

He handed her the extra burrito and drink he bought earlier. She walked out the door into the parking lot, brushing by her so-called friends where they were chatting up some men who were in town promoting a new brand of beer. She walked away from the mayhem towards her dorm room, dialing her spiritual mentor as she went.

Jesus watched her disappear down the street. He said to his disciples, "Time to go. It just goes downhill from here." They cleared their table and stuffed their trash on top of the bulging garbage cans by the door. The collection of human refuse along the street was growing rapidly, but none of them were looking for help from the only place they could get it.

Reflections

Proverbs 20:1 Wine is a mocker and beer a brawler; whoever is led astray by them is not wise.

At first glance, this story is about a college town that creates a fake holiday to make money from college students who would be out of town on a traditional party weekend. The town is Manhattan, Kansas, and Fake Patty's Day was created a week before Saint Patty's Day because the real holiday falls on spring break for the schools and university in the area. Originally designed for Kansas State University students, the idea caught on and now draws students from Kansas University a few miles down the road, several community colleges and a growing number of older adults looking to hook up with coeds. This has caused issues with crimes ranging from public drunkenness, theft and vandalism to sexual assault and extreme littering.

Questions for Contemplation

1. College students spending their weekends drinking heavily has become an accepted, and almost expected, part of culture. It has expanded until this is accepted from high school students as well. What are your thoughts about this type of behavior?

2. Alcohol lowers inhibitions in everyone and increases aggression in some personalities. This leads to higher incidences of fighting, vandalism and sexual assault. These lead to stories which make the overconsumption of alcohol more attractive to those who cannot legally drink

alcohol, without being balanced by the consequences of those actions. How do you feel the fines, pregnancies, prison terms and deaths should be used to educate kids starting in Junior High about the realities of alcohol abuse?

3. Drinking wine and other alcoholic beverages has existed for centuries, perhaps tracing back to how the Earth changed after the flood in Noah's time. While there are several verses in the Bible warning against becoming drunk, the only time avoiding alcohol is mentioned relates to people voluntarily forgoing its use for a limited time when taking a religious vow (Numbers 6:1-12, Judges 13:4-7). Does this conflict with what you have been taught about how alcohol should be viewed from a religious standpoint? If so, how?

4. Studies have been made in many different cultures over many decades which show when something is forbidden, it increases the attractiveness of it. Alcohol-related crimes in European countries without minimum drinking ages, where alcohol is a part of family meals for all ages, are significantly lower. This reflects the Israeli cultural approach as well. Minimum drinking ages in the US trace their roots back to the Puritans, and a resurrection of those beliefs led to the Prohibition era. What role do you think forbidding alcohol plays in the growth of the party culture?

5. As you continue reading the story, the main character reveals a history of being sexually abused by her father. There is a growing number of kids reaching college age with a history of abuse from a parent, neighbor and even religious leaders. Most have been told not to talk about their experiences, usually because the person they reported it to refused to believe their stories. While providing a safe and supportive environment is important for people with these backgrounds, they need specifically trained professional help to guide their recoveries. What resources are available for people with this background in your church? Your local community?

Call to action

As with any issue, using common sense is a key part of addressing social issues. I am allergic to penicillin, so it would be foolish for me to ask my doctor for penicillin every time I have a bacterial infection even though it is still one of the most effective antibiotics available. In the same way, it would be foolish for someone with a history of alcohol abuse-or a family history of alcoholism-to deliberately put themselves in harm's way by "testing" their own tolerance.

Many people know about the existence of Alcoholics Anonymous, Al-Anon and Ala-Teen. These programs include acknowledging a Higher Power through the process for them to go to for supernatural assistance, but they do not teach specifically about God or include Christian principles.

Christian-based recovery centers do exist, and the Betty

Ford Center is probably the most famous one. Teen Challenge is a national program with many local centers that is strictly based on Christian principals. If you feel God leading you to help those suffering from alcohol abuse, I encourage you to contact the Teen Challenge or other Christian treatment centers near you to find out how you can assist them with their mission.

11. THE TRUCK STOP

The summer's heat in Commerce City, Colorado shimmered with diesel fumes. The TA truck stop hummed with its usual semi traffic, one of a couple sitting in the middle of Denver's business district. It was fortunate enough to capture a spot by the 270 bypass, about halfway between I 70 and I 75 and right in the middle of all the action.

Most of the loading and unloading had finished for the day, although some warehouses were open twenty-four hours. By the time the truckers had waited in line to get their loads most of their allowed driving time had lapsed. Team drivers just loaded up on fuel and took off on their routes, but solo drivers had to put in their down time before hitting the roads. The large lot filled up quickly, but there was high enough turnover to keep the attendants busy.

Since it was summer there was an active flow of tourists stopping for gas and a quick bite instead of fighting through the side streets looking for somewhere to eat. The Country Pride restaurant inside would never win Michelin stars for creativity or service, but it was hard to beat for large portions of home-style goodness. Speed and access are more important than discriminating appetites when you are on a tight schedule.

There was light chatter over the CB, but most of the conversations happened in the Driver's Lounge. There were the usual discussions about the weather, sports and the latest escapades of the Swift drivers. After a few parking lot sweeps by the police, word came that the Lounge Lizards had arrived so a few drivers went back to their trucks, looking for some evening entertainment. Some of them spotted the women as they went from truck to truck looking for a customer, while the more dis-

crete ones signaled them which cab to go to.

Most of the private vehicles left after about an hour. There was an exception this evening, however. On the far end of the lot a gray passenger van arrived in the middle of the afternoon, and it was still there as the sun fell set behind the Rocky Mountains. The driver was a shady looking character with long hair, what seemed to be gang tattoos and an aggressive attitude. There was a woman with him in the passenger's seat, whose dress and actions suggested more of a prostitute than anything else. She was clearly the driver's companion, and at least partially responsible for whatever they were up to.

Usually when someone stopped, everyone would pile out and make a run for the restrooms while the driver fueled their vehicle. That didn't happen with the van, however. Everyone stayed in the van while the driver fueled up, then went inside for a few minutes to check out the place.

"Hurry up, David!" the girl in the passenger's seat yelled out the window as he was hanging up the fuel nozzle. "We need to go bad!"

When David came out, he moved the van into a fairly isolated parking spot. "It's clear," he said. "Just be careful in there."

The side windows of the van were covered in a dark tint. The girl pointed behind her to someone sitting in the shadows and said, "You. Come on. And don't try anything funny."

David said to her, "If you need anything, Annie, just punch the code into the phone. I'll be in there, and she won't be leaving on her own two feet."

Annie climbed out of the van. A young girl crawled between the front seats of the van and out the door where Annie had been sitting. They went into the truck stop. Just before they went through the front door Annie grabbed her arm and gave it a quick shake. A few minutes later they emerged, walking a little too close to each other to seem normal.

When they got back to the van, Annie opened her door and half shoved her inside. Then she pointed at someone else, and another girl tumbled out. She looked scared and confused as well. She was given the same threat, and they were off to the restroom as fast as her wobbly legs would take her. When they came back, she was a little steadier, but still not quite sure where she was.

The process repeated itself once more. This girl's eyes were bloodshot like she had been crying, and Annie kept a tight grip on her arm as they crossed the parking lot. The girl tried to shake off her hand a couple times by the van, but Annie's grip tightened until she winced and stopped fighting. Annie literally pulled her across the pavement, lecturing her all the way into the building. Their stay was the shortest of the bunch, and neither one looked very happy when they came back to the van.

"Everything ok," David asked?

"Oh, she thought about running away," Annie responded. "Nothing I couldn't handle, though. Now can we get something to eat?"

"Ok," David said. "We have another hour to kill, so we might as well eat something."

He got out of the van and went back into the truck stop. Business had picked up while they were there, so half an hour had passed when he came back loaded with chicken strips and sweet tea from Popeye's. After he handed out the food, he checked his phone.

"No rush after all," David sighed. "They are caught in a traffic jam and won't be here until later."

There wasn't much conversation in the van. One would expect everyone to be busy tapping on their phones in this situation, but the driver and his companion were the only ones who had one. The other girls shifted restlessly in their seats, occasionally digging into their bags to stare at something for a few minutes before shoving it back. The one who had been crying earlier started sniffling again, but David immediately screamed at her and it came to an abrupt halt.

As if on cue, his phone rang again. After a few terse words, he hung up and slammed it into the arm rest.

"What is it, David," Annie asked?

"They still haven't cleaned up the accident yet. We are going to be stuck here even longer," he replied.

"That isn't fair," she wailed. 'We should have been back in Salt Lake City by then. Freddie promised his best customers the new girls tonight!"

"I'm sure it's the same story on the other end," he said. "Somehow this driver always manages to be hours late, and his excuses don't always check out. I'm surprised he hasn't been replaced yet."

"Well, it is Angel's brother," Annie snorted. "I guess he can get away with sampling the merchandise and breaking the schedule when nobody else can."

"Speaking of which, we've already lost money on this trip. If they are going to be that late, I think it's time we took advantage of the situation. Take one of the girls into the lounge and see what you can get for her," David said.

"Sounds good to me," Annie said. She turned around and pointed to the most cooperative girl. "Come on. It's time you saw some action."

The girl clearly wanted nothing to do with this, but she was more scared of what they would do to her than any man in the truck stop. She had run away from being abused by her neighbor, so she had some experience at least. As she crawled out of the van, she smiled at the other two. "At least it isn't you, yet," she half whispered.

When Annie heard that, she turned to David as she was shutting the door. "If I find anyone that wants to mess with clueless and crybaby, I'll send them out here."

David gave her a thumb up, and watched them walk into the station. Traffic had eased up a bit and the overnight lot was full, so it was easier to track where they went. After the mandatory restroom stop to fix the girl's makeup and clothes, they went into the Trucker's Lounge to try to drum up some business.

It wasn't long before they headed out to a blue Peterbilt with a balding man who outweighed both of them. Two

MR. PHILIP LEON BROWN

long-haired men in their thirties followed them out, and Annie
pointed them towards the van.

"Showtime, girls," David yelled into the back. "And if either one of you give me issues, so help me, neither one of you
will leave this van alive. Do I make myself clear?"

The girls had heard threats like this before, but they had
come to believe him. There were quick rustles of clothes being
adjusted, and the snap of lipstick and compact lids followed.
They looked more like two teenagers clumsily getting ready
for their Friday night dates than the promised prostitutes they
were supposed to be, but sometimes reality sneaks in no matter
how hard you try to disguise it.

Annie reached the truck about the same time the two
men got to the van. As Annie and her girl climbed into the cab,
David rolled down the window of the van.

"Yes," he asked? "What do you want?"

"I'm Jesus, and this is my buddy John," Jesus said. "Annie
over there said we should come over here for some entertainment."

"Are you two cops," David asked?

"No, we don't have that kind of authority," Jesus replied.
"Now convince me we didn't waste our time coming over here."

"Well, for one hundred dollars you can do anything you
want to these girls for an hour," David said. "They are new, so it
will be worth your while."

"And they are in a filthy van without any beds," Jesus answered. "How many drugs have you been taking to think they
are worth that?"

"Ok, ok," David said. "Make it fifty. But you don't get into
the van until I have the money."

Jesus motioned to John, who pulled out a handful of twenties and gave it to the man. David quickly opened the door to
the van and motioned them in. "Don't dawdle," he mumbled.

The girls awkwardly stood up and Jesus climbed into the
van. When he stopped in the passenger's seat, David started to
get flustered.

"Sit down, David," Jesus said. "Your job is done."

David tried to stand up and reach for his gun, but he couldn't move. The more he struggled, the more helpless he was. Finally, he stammered out, "Just wait until Annie gets over here. Whatever you are trying to pull will be all over then."

Jesus smiled at him and said, "Oh, she is already on her way back. It seems the trucker they went to developed some, how shall we say, difficulties and changed his mind."

Jesus turned back to the girls. "Hang on a minute. The other two are almost here."

A minute later, Annie and her charge were at the van. Jesus moved out of the door and helped them through the door where he had been standing. Annie was laughing hysterically about the trucker, while the girl just looked relieved. When David didn't respond as she expected, she stopped laughing and took in the situation.

"Hey, what's going on," Annie asked? "Are you still negotiating over these two, or are you discussing politics? They should be inside going at it by now."

"Oh, we're going to get to it," Jesus replied. "Your friend is a little tongue-tied right now, but we were waiting for you."

"You better not start something, because I have a gun and I'm not afraid to use it," she said.

"We are starting something right now," Jesus said. "Now sit down and behave yourself. You might as well get used to it where you are going. We don't have much time, so listen carefully."

Annie reached towards her purse but found herself slumping into the passenger seat with the girls instead. She, too, made several futile attempts to take back control of the situation before realizing she was as helpless as David.

Jesus pointed to the girl who kept crying first. "Kim, you can stop crying now. Your prayers have been heard, and they are the same as your Grandmothers'. In a few minutes you will be on your way back home to her. Hopefully now you will understand why you have the rules she set out for you and follow them."

'Thank you," Kim replied. "I understand now."

"You're not going anywhere," David muttered under his breath.

"Mikala, it's time for you to go back home. Your neighbor is going to be in jail soon, so you will be safe. Just promise me that you will be brave and tell the police what he did to you so he will go away for a long time.

"I will, sir," Mikala replied. "I won't know how to live without worrying about him,"

"I'm sure you asked for it," David sniffed.

Jesus turned to face the last girl in the van. "Candace, go back home and live the life you know to be right. Your life is about knowing who you are in God's eyes, not in how you dress or wear makeup. Outer beauty is only temporary. Who you are inside is what draws the right people into your life. Just focus on being who God made you to be, and you will find success in your life."

Candace smiled at him and said," Thank you. I feel like such a fraud when I act like the popular crowd."

"Too bad you will never find out how much money you can get using your pretty face," Annie snorted.

"Well, it's time for us to get on down the road. Just hang tight for a few more minutes and everything will work itself out," Jesus told the girls.

Jesus backed out of the van and closed the passenger door where he had been leaning in. He put a hand on John's shoulder, and they began walking back to the station as if nothing had happened.

As soon as the door closed, David tried lunging towards the gun under his seat and Annie turned to give the girls in the back seat a piece of her mind for believing the garbage Jesus had told them. Both discovered they were still restrained by the same invisible force they experienced while Jesus was there. Not only were their bodies tied to the seats, they weren't able to talk, either. They sat there and fumed while the girls in the back moved to gather their things, somehow fully expecting

the things Jesus told them to take place.

When Jesus and John reached the front of the station, they turned around. A white cargo van screeched into the parking spot where they had been standing moments before. After a few moments, a man with long, greasy hair and a vest with a gang logo on the back got out of the driver's seat and walked to the grey van. After a few minutes' conversation both side doors, now facing each other, opened. As the three girls from the gray van came out, three exited the white van.

Before the girls began climbing into the new vans to complete the exchange, four black sedans surrounded them with flashing lights. The delay hadn't been an accident. The white van had been caught in a DUI checkpoint and identified as a potential human trafficking vehicle. The bust had been set up and based on the information they provided, and it was now happening. Six victims and four perpetrators were taken off the streets that night.

As a bonus, the local police had strategically positioned themselves around the parking lot before the bust began. They captured two pimps and four Lounge Lizards as they attempted to run away. After searching the trucks on the overnight lot, two more women and three boys were picked up. The human trafficking business had taken a hit, but there was more work to be done.

Reflections

Ezekiel 16:15 "'But you trusted in your beauty and used your fame to become a prostitute. You lavished your favors on anyone who passed by and your beauty became his.

Human trafficking is a large and growing problem. It has many faces as well. While prostitution used to be fueled with either people voluntarily practicing it or forcing runaways to do the work, times have changed. Now the trade is supplied from

things as varied as luring kids through the internet for relationships and recruiting for high-paying jobs to kidnapping people
off the street to parents pimping their own children. While the
trade used to mainly use women and girls, boys and men are
likely to be targets now as well.

Those who are lured over the internet are typically unhappy with their home life. This is difficult to counter, since
that is part of the typical teenage experience. Those who run
away from home take this to a higher level, and for good reason.
Runaways frequently have experienced physical or sexual abuse
or neglect, as well. Whatever their background, there is some
aspect of being unhappy with their home life.

Prostitution also has a high correlation with drug abuse
and alcoholism. While some voluntarily turn to drugs as a way
to deal with their lifestyles, that is not always the case. Kidnap
victims and runaways are frequently forced to become addicts
as an easy way to control them in their new lifestyles.

Questions for Contemplation

1. Prostitution and human trafficking is more common
   in urban areas than rural ones. However, rural areas
   are frequently easier areas to get new victims from
   because of increased dissatisfaction with living in a
   small town and a greater tendency to trust people.
   How many teenagers and young adults have disappeared from your community? How successful have
   efforts been to recover them?

2. One key to deterring internet relationships recruiting
   teens to leave their parents is for parents to strictly
   control not only internet time, but to monitor who

their kids are contacting. This is more difficult because there are apps that mask who they are contacting. If you have kids at home, how successful are you in fulfilling your parenting role of monitoring who they are friends with?

3. Many victims of human trafficking are reluctant to go back home because of shame and the bad experiences they had there. What role can you play to intervene in unhealthy homes to deter kids from running away from them?

4. Prostitutes quickly become hopeless and jaded about life, especially if they are addicts. How can they be approached in ways that give them hope for the future to pull them out of their lifestyles?

5. Churches and ministries can play a positive role in reaching prostitutes by reaching out to them and providing them food and medical help. What ministries or churches in your area actively reach out to human trafficking victims?

Call to Action

The first step to stopping human trafficking is to make sure you aren't contributing to the problem. If there is abuse in your home, put an end to it. If your child is showing hostility or withdrawal, get them professional help. If someone tells you about being abused by a neighbor or relative have the situation investigated instead of just blowing it off. If someone is engaged with porn or prostitutes, have an intervention and hold them accountable for stopping the behavior.

The next step is to treat everyone as equals. If you know someone who is a prostitute, show them love instead of condemning them. If you know a teen or young adult who is talking or acting out sexually, walk beside them to show them a better way. Threatening and condemning someone in high school and college is ineffective, so follow Christ's instructions to love them like you love yourself.

There are ministries out there who reach out to human trafficking victims and prostitutes. One is the Dream Center in Los Angeles, California. Another one is Mercy Ministries, which is associated with Joyce Meyer. XXX is a ministry with several outreach programs across the US. There is one ministry in Manhattan, Kansas I don't remember the name of that led to at least two strip clubs being shut down by taking gift baskets to the workers there and ministering to them. Contact your local church to find out what ministries in your area reach out to human trafficking victims.

12. THE GAME

Tree City Church was built on dreams. A dream that the church should be an important part of the community, even when it wasn't Sunday. A dream that it should be the first place a person having problems should think of for help. A dream that it should be a focal point for kids looking for something to do after school and on the weekends. A dream their main meeting space should be flexible enough to hold basketball games, concerts and events instead of being pinned into place by pews screwed into the floor. A welcoming place who cared enough for their community to allow people with differing views a place to reach out to others for the common good.

With a dream that big, the only things needed to make it a reality was land and money. A lot of land and a lot of money. With a growing congregation from several thriving communities feeding the building fund kitty, the financial end of things began to come into focus.

Now for the land part of it. With the state capital and main university, Boise was thriving-despite having bright blue turf in their college stadium. Tucked between Lake Lowell with its water sports on one side and the mountains on the other, the rest is surrounded by enough fields of potatoes and garlic to feed the masses. The varied businesses and recreational opportunities make it a magnet for families looking to put down roots.

There was a strip of undeveloped land buffering Boise from Meridian, a thriving community in its own right and home to several members of the congregation. They looked into buying an old farm being squeezed out from both cities to hold a church large enough for community groups to utilize. In front of the church there would be room enough to develop fields for playing football and soccer. It was the perfect location but being able to make the deal happen was another matter.

When something is God's will, every impossible situation is just another chance for a miracle. Agreeable terms were met, and a contract signed between the church board and Pastor Stickney. Ground was broken within weeks of the design being approved, and the church was off and running.

Then came the waiting. Months and months of waiting. After agonizing over the perfect design, construction brought a few twists and turns as it always does. The ground had a couple surprises. Drainage didn't quite work like it was supposed to. That big area for kids to play turned into a bog that just wouldn't dry up. All par for the course with a construction project that size, but it was a stifling damper to those waiting to see their dreams of outreach and community involvement come to fruition.

Finally, the building was finished. The walls and ceiling passed inspection, and the dressing up began. Nice neutral colors were selected for the auditorium/gymnasium and most of the rooms below. Some not-so-neutral colors went into the children's rooms, with murals of Bible stories on at least one wall of each classroom. The teen area had colors that were, shall we say, designed more to wake the walking dead than to provide aesthetics.

Laying the carpet took a couple weeks. Preparing the floor of the main meeting and activity room took even longer. It is not easy to prepare a floor with great traction for athletic events, yet sturdy enough to be pounded by chairs, tables and the random props necessary to operate efficiently with the smallest footprints possible.

The months of construction expanded into preparation. The community outreach effort began with a huge marketing blitz to the surrounding area for their first services. It was a resounding success, and several new families began attending as a result.

The media blitz had a second goal as well. The local

neighborhoods weren't the only ones targeted with their welcoming message. Official letters were sent to community groups looking for a safe place to meet, followed by meetings with staff and encouragement from the members who were a part of them. It wasn't just the pretty groups with good reputations, either. Soon the church became a place where not only scouts of all sorts meet, but also AA, Al-Anon and mental health groups as well. The dream of meeting the needs of the community were turning into reality.

The whirlwind of people using the church every day of the week settled into as much of a routine as that sort of thing allowed. The groups came and went, and a few times a year, special events like concerts or special speakers tried to draw them into a more cohesive community. Leaders came and went, but the strength of the dream persevered to help everyone through the good times and rough spots as well.

There was one part of the dream that remained unfulfilled, however. While adults were getting spiritual guidance through the groups they attended and the children learned life skills in scouting and AWANA groups, a void still existed. There still weren't organized sports to keep the kids distracted and learning more life skills and Christian disciplines outside of the teen and kid programs.

One of the active members coached at a local high school. Not only did he have a passion for kids, he had a couple children of his own and understood the need for wholesome activities for them. The new pastor Tim Goodfellow had just learned of a Christian-based sports program they could plug into for support and technical advice. All the pieces seemed to be falling into place to make the last part of their outreach dream a reality.

Pastor Goodfellow connected with Mark and his wife Anna in late spring. They met at Westside Drive Inn for one of the best hamburgers in the state, followed by their famous Baked Potato ice cream sundaes. Between the sugar shock and the food coma, the pastor broached the subject. After discussing it for a while and tossing around a few ideas, the couple decided to pray about it and give him an answer in a few days.

Mark and Anna followed up with Pastor Goodfellow the next week. They decided to explore the program and make a final decision after they had more information. Three years later they were on their way to Chicago to the annual Upward convention to find out more about this crazy idea they had at least temporarily signed up to be a part of.

Something at the convention got them excited. It may have been the extra humidity and oxygen they were breathing in Chicago, but whatever it was their excitement followed them home. They met with the pastor and started planning to make the program a reality at their church.

One of the first steps was also the most difficult. Mark resigned his full-time coaching position at the high school because of the time commitment it would take. It was a difficult step, but a teaching position opened at their junior high for him. Contracts were signed and the goodbyes said. With that level of commitment, it was full speed ahead from that point.

They had set up a network of teams with an association in Nampa before becoming involved with Upward. With the teams and coaches already in place, it was a matter of letting them know the new policies and expectations of the new program. After several coaches' meetings and more paperwork completed, the Upward Bound program became a reality at Tree City with thirty-two teams and two hundred sixty kids in their basketball and cheerleading league.

Most of the players had been together in the other league, and their chemistries were good. There was one team, called the Raptors, made up of the leftovers-kids who wanted to play but were new to the league and did not have a team to join. It was the most challenging team for two reasons. First, the players did not know each other and did not have any experience playing together. Second, the parents were, for the most part, not die-hard fans like the other teams so their cheering section wasn't as strong as the others.

Attendance picked up at the Raptor games a couple weeks into the season, however. There were a group of men in town for three months helping out the Lighthouse Men's Mission. Somehow they heard of the team and looked up their schedule. From that point on at least some of them were there to cheer on the players every game.

Friendships quickly formed between the men and the players. This was aided somewhat with the treats they brought. Even though they only brought a small bag from the Alberstons down the road, there was always plenty of snacks for everyone and extra for their opponents. As the season progressed, the men and players began spending time together in the lobby after their games. The time bonding and learning each other's strengths helped the team to grow enough so they began winning some of their games as well.

On one particularly rough night, the Raptors were defeated by fifty points. A loss that bad defeated them in their hearts and minds as well as on the court. Some of the kids headed straight for the door after the loss, heads hanging low, the pain of the loss greater than the usual teen hunger pangs. Judas and Thomas made a quick dash to redirect them to the lobby for their usual post-game snacks. Even the most depressed were won over when ice cream Drumsticks and Tropicana pouches came out of the bag.

When the snacks had been handed out and the sugar started easing the pain of defeat, the leader sat in the middle of their chairs and began talking to them. The pep talks by the coach lay in the dust of history. This time it was a wise friend reaching out, not only to the players but the parents and coach as well.

"It was a rough night out there," Jesus began. "Even though you played hard, nothing seemed to go your way."

Several of the boys nodded in agreement. Even when they followed the play exactly, something seemed to go wrong. Either the ball bounced in a weird direction, someone's shoe slipped, or a player from the other team appeared in the wrong spot. Even the ball from the game on the court next to them kept flying over and creating chaos.

"This is one of the toughest teams in the league," Jesus continued. "They are bigger, faster, and have played together for a couple years. The important thing is you stayed out there and followed the game plan until the end."

"Scott, this is the hardest you have played all year. Each time you were caught off guard you learned from your mistake, and you didn't fall for that move again."

"Alex, I've never seen you run as fast as you did tonight. At first your opponent was running circles around you. Instead of giving up you kept trying harder, and you were keeping up with him by the end of the game."

"Every one of you grew tonight as you struggled with someone who had more experience. Even though you didn't win tonight, the things you learned playing against this team will help you as you play against other teams in the future."

"That's the way life is sometimes. When everything seems to be going against you, that is when you learn to fight and have faith. You learn the most important things when everything seems to be going wrong, and those things will be what makes you successful the rest of your life."

"Just to show you how the best things can come when everything seems to be going badly, I have a surprise for you tonight. There is a bag for each of you to take home tonight. Don't open it until you get home, though. You can tell me what you think about it after the next game, ok?"

After they chatted for a while, everyone bundled up and went out into the cold March air. They each opened their bag when they got home, and it was something the whole family liked. They talked about what was in the bag when they saw each other again, and it helped them stay focused as they practiced.

The team's successes and the joy they had playing together caught the attention of the player's parents. Their cheering section grew, and the parents began to get to know each other, as well. The community environment of the program, along with the halftime devotionals that were a part of the program, drew some of them to begin coming to church as well. Finally, the dream of involving the children in wholesome activities after church had become a reality.

At the end of the season, the Upward Bound program had a big banquet for all of the players, coaches and volunteers. It was the last time the men would see their favorite team, but they celebrated their friendships and growth together. After the meal, Bruce Crevier talked and showed them some trick basketball moves, both entertaining and challenging them to remember the things they had learned over the season.

There were hugs and tears after the banquet. The kids and their families headed home, thinking about finishing school and the summer to come. The men headed back to where they had been staying to pack up so they could drive to their next job in the morning. The program was already a success, not only for providing an activity for the community kids after school, but also for helping them grow and learn more about what it meant to be a Christian.

Reflections

Deuteronomy 6:6-8 These commandments that I give you today are to be on your hearts. Impress them on your children. Talk about them when you sit at home and when you walk along the road, when you lie down and when you get up.

Engaging children in after-school and summer programs is an effective way to keep them from joining gangs or other detrimental groups. These elements range from spending hours playing video games to online bullying to groups pushing drug abuse, terrorist recruitment, suicide pacts and murder. While consistent positive parenting plays an important role in deterring these types of interests, a majority of children spend at least part of their day alone due to parent's work schedules or other commitments.

Churches without a recreation area generally focus on scouting programs like AWANA and the Boy Scouts or have tutoring or mentoring programs to keep children involved with positive activities. Those with gyms or multi-purpose rooms can use sports or other physical activities to keep the kids involved. No matter the size of the community or church, there are options available to help teach kids in your community the values of teamwork, responsibility and religious values.

The sports program in this story is a fictionalized story of how my sister Naomi Fulwood and her husband Tim built the Upward sports program in Tree City Church in Boise, Idaho. The number of kids and teams they started with is accurate. Since then they have expanded into several other communities and other sports as well. They are currently in the process of developing a club league for higher level athletes with the same dedication to Christian values and sportsmanship.

Questions for Contemplation

1. The negative influences facing children vary with where they live and the culture they know. What are the major influences facing them in your community?

2. Does your church provide any programs that have a positive influence on kids during the week? If so, how effective is it?

3. In order to positively influence kids, a program has to be culturally relevant to them. What changes could be made to your programs so they would be more at-

tractive to kids outside of your church?

4. Many people think you have to be young or have kids at home to be involved in a children's ministry. In reality Senior Citizens play a key role in effective kids outreach programs since they generally have more time to spend, have more life experiences to share their knowledge from and add stability in leadership. How can you integrate your Senior Citizens into your children's programs to maximize their value?

5. All children's programs take a lot of time, energy and financial resources to stay viable. What areas in your church's programs are the weakest, and how can you help fill in their gaps?

Call to Action

Each community and church have their own unique challenges. There are common needs everywhere, though. The main issue is having enough volunteers to care for the kids who attend. After that there are financial needs not just for supplies and equipment, but also to cover the utilities additional time in facilities cause. The most effective programs involve community outreach, so funds need to be raised to cover these activities and volunteers recruited who know how to perform the work being done.

There are many organizations focused on helping kids grow up in a Christ-centered environment. AWANA is a scout-type program focused on scripture memorization I attended growing up and still have several medals from. Kids Hope and Youth for Christ are organizations that work through elementary, junior high and high schools. Upward is the nationwide sports program this story is based on. Other Christian-based sports groups include Youth for Christ, Fellowship of Christian Athletes, Church Sports and Recreational Ministries, Christian Sports International, Christian Outdoor Fellowship of America and Hooked for Life. No matter what type of activities the kids in your area are interested in, somewhere there is Christian outreach group who will help you keep them interested and active.

13. THE CENTER

Carina Vasquez shifted slightly against the concrete wall of her room in the Adelanto ICE Processing Center. Her back ached from years of picking crops, moving from strawberries to olives to pistachios to apples as the seasons changed. Most of her life had been spent rotating between work camps, with occasional trips back across the border to her family land outside San Agustin Lanquin, Guatemala.

She grew up on the family farm. She was young when they sold the timber and the land was clear cut. They kept a small herd of cows, grazing them on open pasture with the other farmers in the region. Each family grew a garden by their homes, selling any extra produce at the market in town. She looked forward to market days, where she played with the other children and ate different foods from farms in the river valley.

Survival was more important than education, so she learned how to tend the crops and care for the livestock instead of going to school. She helped harvest and prepare food for her extended family. Carina was adventurous and became known for finding new edibles in the forest and using them in her cooking. Her talents attracted the attention of Miguel, one of the most respected leaders in the area, and they were married in the Catedral De Lanquin while they were teenagers.

Three tones on the intercom interrupted Carina's memories. The voice announced comida was being served. She ignored the words, having gone through the same routine three times a day since they had been brought here two months ago. She automatically called to her children Ana and Antonio, who were playing with the other children in the small clear area in the middle of the room. Nobody would be served until all the children were standing with their mother so they could be checked off the list at the front of the table. Corina and the kids picked up their trays with a bowl of chicken, rice and a tortilla and sat down on their blankets to eat. Even though meals were typically the social center for Central Americans the room was quiet while they ate. There was simply nothing new to talk about.

Meals for detainees were consistent since they were on a strict budget and there were over three thousand in a center designed for less than two thousand. The lure of higher pay always drew thousands of illegal immigrants across the border. The rumor of lax immigration enforcement and increased benefits for non-citizens fueled the drive, especially for parents sending unaccompanied minors to a better place to live. Unfortunately, the rumors proved to be untrue, and the clumsy process for documenting detainees and returning them to their countries was several months behind schedule. Tracing families down to release children to their families did little to relieve pressure on the system since many of their relatives were also in the country illegally, or there were not any relatives to release them to.

The smell of food from Cross Eyed Cow Pizza drifted out of the break room where the staff was eating. Even though most of the detainees ate traditional food, the smell of food from the outside mocked their inability to eat as they wanted. Carl's Jr or Bravo Burgers nearby were also favorites of the workers. Even the occasional smell of home-made lasagna fueled their desire for something other than the predictable soup or stew.

When they were finished eating, Corina returned the trays and dishes to the cart. When everyone was finished, they were returned to the central kitchen for cleaning. All the kids had to stay on their blankets until the cart was gone, since it took up most of the space that was not covered with blankets for sleeping. Antonio was still young enough to take a nap after lunch, and Ana had to stay with him to make sure he was not disturbed and to guard their belongings.

After Antonio fell asleep, Corina went over to the restrooms to make sure chaos did not break out. There were two open stalls, each with a toilet at the bottom and sink directly above it. The supply of toilet paper was limited, so it was important to make sure nobody wasted it or used it for other things. It was also important to limit the amount used to prevent the toilets from clogging, especially since they tended to be finicky on their best days.

The after-meal restroom ritual concluded without mishap, and Corina walked to their assigned patch of floor. She stood on edge of the blanket closest to the play area and told Ana she could play with the others again. The building supervisor had assigned each mother a time to watch the children so everyone would get a break, and it was her group's turn. One took out the box of blocks to build things with. Another flipped through the pile of coloring books looking for pages that hadn't been used yet. Some of the children sat down at Corina's feet, waiting for her to tell them stories of what it was like when she grew up.

This day she told them about the time she climbed the mountain looking for a special mushroom and was chased by a panther. She escaped by running to where the bulldozers were clearing the forest. As she was walking back to her home, she found a large stand of chicory she hung up to dry to make tea with. She had a knack for storytelling, so this distracted the kids for over an hour.

Carina enjoyed telling the children stories of her home, but it also made her a little sad. She would still be in that village, raising her children as Miguel on their family farm, if they had not been driven out by the Sinaloa Cartel. They appeared first by organizing local gangs of thieves to attack the tourists on their way to the Semuc Champey Falls and the Kanba Cave. They soon moved to take over local businesses and had pressured farmers to begin growing their drugs. When farmers who did not cooperate began to disappear, they decided it was better to risk picking crops in the United States and sending the money back to their village to support those who fought the cartel. It was risky, especially with children, but it was safer than fighting the cartel themselves.

At four o'clock the intercom toned again. It was time for the daily cleaning and restocking ritual. Everyone who slept on the floor had to roll up their blankets and walk along the exercise area while the staff cleaned and disinfected it. All four caged areas had to be prepared, but Carina's group were usually the first one. While the unfortunate ones walked around clutching their belongings, those who had bunks would often steal toilet paper and other supplies from the storage areas after they were refilled, forcing everyone else to use what was left. The staff tried to prevent this from happening and frequently searched those usually responsible before leaving the cage, but they were not always successful in their efforts.

Today the cleaning took longer than usual. There seemed to be an urgency in the process as well. When they could lay their blankets back down on the cold gray floors, they were told to make sure everything was neat and looked good. Apparently, there would be visitors before supper was served, and there would be consequences if things were messy or anyone complained too much about the sleeping arrangements or food.

It was announced cena would be served later than usual because the guests were taking a long time to process. All the visitors and everything they brought were searched, and the boxes x-rayed for weapons. The children started to get antsy, since the staff had removed the books and coloring sheets to prevent anyone from giving the guests notes.

The doors finally swung open, and the guests filtered in. Only three guests were allowed into each section with a staff member, and each team brought three boxes with them. They set the boxes on the tables set up to serve food on, and the children crowded as close as they dared to see what the strangers brought.

As the boxes were opened, one of the staff read a short statement over the intercom. The strangers were from Desert Springs Baptist Church, a few blocks from the Center. They

wanted the detainees to know they were praying for them and had brought them a few things to make their stay a little more pleasant. There were a few more pleasantries mixed in, but there was far more interest in what they had brought than making friends with people they would probably never see again.

The first box they opened was for the kids. The top was full of new coloring books, crayons, artist pads and paints. The rest of the box was full of dolls, Lego sets, puzzles and Bibles in Spanish for the ladies. The kids were allowed to look at the toys, but the staff quickly put everything back in the box to keep the area clear for the food.

The second box was opened. There was an eclectic mixture of socks and underwear in it, followed by a variety of personal hygiene items. Once again one of the guests held up a few of the items to show everyone what was available, before the staff made him put everything back in the box to be distributed later.

It was the third box that was gained the most attention, however. It was full of fruit from the tropics. There were avocados, mangos, guavas, tamarillos and platanos to choose from. The fruit would be a welcome taste of home after the bland food they were served from the center kitchen. The box of fruit was placed at the end of the food line to be served with cena.

The food was wheeled in and set up on the tables. The visitors stayed to serve and were given instructions on how much to give everyone while the families lined up together. After each family was checked off, the visitors helped dish out the food and made small talk with them as they moved down the table. The last stop was the box of fruit, where everyone was allowed to take one to go with their meal.

The one who served the rice was the most memorable. His hair was long, threatening to escape from the standard hair net issued by the center. His beard was long as well, and it was covered by not one but two nets. His eyes appeared to bulge out a bit, probably an illusion caused by his ears forced away from his head by three sets of strings. The twinkle in his brown eyes offset his caricaturist appearance, though. While the guests serving the chicken stew and tortillas struggled a bit to talk as they served, he bantered easily as he served and seemed to know what to say to each one.

When the trays were emptied and stacked with the pots on the cart, the staff took what remained of the boxes of fruit back to the kitchen. The box of toys was placed on one table and the one called Jesus sorted out the books. The kids were allowed to choose one, either coloring or reading, and take one Bible for each family. The remaining toys were stacked with the communal toys in the stand in the corner to be checked out during the scheduled play times.

The one called Simon and Mary from the church sorted the underwear and hygiene items out on the other table. The mothers sorted through the clothes and took one set for each child and for herself. When everyone in each room had gone through their box, the staff made a list of any missing sizes and went into the other rooms to find enough for everyone. Everyone got their own toothpaste, a new toothbrush and a deodorant. Once again anything remaining was combined into the boxes and taken into the storeroom to be given out later.

Carina picked through the pile of socks and underwear, relieved for her kids to have something to replace theirs that were growing thin from being worn so much. They were also becoming too small because of their growth during the time they had been detained. She found some for herself, the first she had gotten in some time because of her sacrifices for the kids. She picked out some things from the personal hygiene items, then moved over to the toy table so her kids could pick out a book.

As the kids were going over the books, she noticed some of them were not in Spanish. Her kids may understand them from the schooling they had gone through, but she would never be able to help read them. When Ana began flipping through one of the books in English, she called out to her.

"Ana, choose another one. I can not help you read that one," Carina warned.

"But Mama, I like the pictures in this one," Ana plead. "And it's about cats."

"I know, nina," Carina answered. "But I can not help you rea it since it's in English."

Ana reluctantly put the book down, but kind of off to the side so she knew where it was. She began looking through the rest of the stack, but without much enthusiasm.

"Madre, what is the matter," Jesus asked?

"It is the book, senor," Carina answered. "Ana loves cats, and she misses hers since we are kept in here."

"I understand," Jesus said. "How long have you been kept in here?

Carina said softly, "It has been more than three months, and we still haven't had a hearing yet. Our clothes are getting worn, and our family is afraid to come see us.

"Your family has not forgotten you," Jesus said. "They are trying to get you and Miguel released so you can be a family again."

Jesus smiled at her. "I know you do, and I'm listening. Just a few more days and you will be together again."

"From your lips to God, senor," Carina said, a little light of hope returning to her eyes. "I know we're not supposed to ask you this, but could you try to contact my family and see what they need to get us released?"

"It is already on my list of things to do," Jesus replied. "Is Frederik and Gloria still working at Thermal?

"Yes, they should be," Carina replied. Then her jaw dropped, and she stared at the stranger in disbelief. "Wait a minute, how did you know my brother's name and where he is working?"

"Oh, you would be surprised at what I know," Jesus answered. "Like they are about to tell your kids to pick something and go sit down so the rest of the children can pick their books."

On cue, one of the staff not known for being pleasant walked over to the table and told her kids to pick out a book and move on, or they would not get to have one. She stood there with her hands on her hips glaring at them to make sure they got the point.

Antonio was a little afraid of her from past confrontations, so he quickly grabbed one of the coloring books in front of him and rushed to Corina's side. Ana still hesitated over the choices, still desperately wanting to take the book about cats.

"Here, I think you will like this one Ana," Jesus said. He reached over and picked up the one about cats and handed it to her.

Ana reached out to take it, saw which one it was, and drew her hands back. "Senor, I can not take it because it is not in Spanish," she said. There was a little tremor in her voice, and tears were not far away.

"Oh, I think you were looking at the one next to it," Jesus answered with a little chuckle. "See here, this is the same book, but this one is written in Spanish. Go ahead, take it with you."

Ana and Carina both looked at the book, and it was the story about Cats. In Spanish. With all of those beautiful pictures of different kinds of cats she fell in love with. Carina quickly looked back at the table, and there was not another book about cats anywhere to be seen. Somehow, when Jesus picked up the book the words changed languages.

Ana quickly took the book and thanked Jesus for his help finding it. Carina just shook her head, put an arm around each one of her children, and herded them back to their blanket to see their new things. The grumpy staff member had no idea what had happened, did not care, and simply turned around and yelled at the next family to hurry up and pick their toys so she could chase the visitors out and make everyone get ready to sleep.

Reflections

Hebrews 13:2 Do not forget to show hospitality to strangers, for by so doing some people have shown hospitality to angels without knowing it.

Of all the stories in this book, there is probably more reasons for people to get upset in this one. It is one I struggled with including for several months and was the next to the last chapter I wrote. The topic just would not go away, even though I do not know more than the a few words of Spanish and have never been close to fields picked by hand other than my garden.

You may be offended that I called them illegal aliens. This is the correct legal term for people who cross the border without permission, no matter what country you live in. The term "undocumented immigrants" and "dreamers" are euphemisms designed to create sympathy for people in this situation. Part of being a good neighbor and serving those around us is being honest about who they are.

You may be offended that I did not talk about the rights of illegal aliens. By definition, people who enter a country illegally do not have any rights under the constitution of that country. They do not have rights, but the United States is one of a handful of nations who have created a system for them be granted green cards under specific conditions instead of being returned to their homelands. While this may seem harsh, it is again part of the process of understanding who they are the legal process they must go through to be granted the right to stay here.

You may be offended that I included illegal aliens in this book as your neighbors. We know there are millions of them living in the United States, and they are not just found around undesirable jobs such as harvesting crops by hand or working in meat packing plants. It would be difficult to find an area where there is not at least one family within a fifty-mile radius.

Another issue many people have with detention centers is they separate families. In reality, they do this because of laws passed by Congress and state legislators. Any detention center funded with federal or state funds, including jails and homeless shelters, are required by law to house men separately from women and children.

Questions for Contemplation:

1. Illegal aliens choose to bypass the immigration process to live and work in United States. Some of those who cross the border are criminals fleeing from prosecution and gang members infiltrating local criminal organizations. How does the low number of criminals affect how you view the rest of those who cross the borders illegally?

2. Four years ago I would have said that all illegal immigrants should be deported immediately unless they could prove they were fleeing wars at home. Since then I have learned that the parable of the good neighbor in Luke 10 did not have a caveat to exclude those who have crossed the border without permission. In what ways has nationalism or patriotism clouded your willingness to help those in need?

3. There is a tendency to be friends with people like yourself, because you can understand them better and have similar interests. This can easily be used as an excuse to avoid those from other cultures, especially those in lower socio-economic conditions. This is often a convenient cover to excuse racism or believing at some level those of another race are inferior mentally, physically or economically because of their genetics. Carefully consider how you view those of other races and list any races or sexualities you have show bias towards.

4. On the other side of the coin, there are those who say we should have open borders and let anyone who wants to live in the US. While claiming to base this on the Biblical principal of loving your neighbors, it ignores the entire Old Testament which documents the Israelites fighting many wars to maintain their borders. It also ignores the law that forced any foreigner who wanted to join the Israelites to be circumcised and follow the Jewish religion. Does this reminder of Jewish history change your perspective on open borders?

5. Do you know of any churches or Christian outreaches in your area that focus on providing legal or support services to illegal aliens? Do you know of any outreach programs in your area, such as food banks, who refuse to serve illegal aliens?

Call to Action:

Illegal aliens probably represent the most isolated segment of society. They are isolated from their extended families, or from all of their relatives if they cross the border alone. Many are isolated by language, since a large percentage come from areas where their primary language is Spanish or local dialects and English is rarely heard. They are isolated socially and culturally, except for the camps or small communities they temporarily called home. They are isolated legally, since reporting crimes can lead to their own deportation-which has a tendency to cause the criminal element to be more active. They can also be the victims of racism as mentioned in question three above.

There are some Christian outreach groups focused on being neighbors to illegal aliens. Once is the ISAAC project (https://isaacproject.org/about-us), a project between Baylor University and one of the Baptist organizations. Based out of Texas, it focuses on providing a Christian perspective on immigration issues. This includes giving English as a Second Language (ESL) classes, citizenship and other literacy classes. They also provide legal advice to help them avoid being preyed on by those who scam them out of money for immigration services they fail to provide.

The Embassy Church in Denver (www.theembassy.org) has an outreach program to their local ICE detention center. They visit weekly, providing legal advice and resources to the detainees there to help them navigate the immigration process. They also provide services to the homeless and their local homeless shelters.

National Justice for our Neighbors (https://njfon.org/) is an outreach of the Methodist Church. They provide legal services to help navigate through the immigration process. Their focus is on keeping families together as they work through the system, which is rare.

Another area of action Christians should become involved in is changing federal and state laws forcing men to be housed separately from women and children. The theory is separating men and women create environments that discourage crime. The reality is crimes still occur in detention facilities, and the damage caused by separating families has not been explored.

If you are interested in helping illegal aliens, please contact the resources above for more information. You should also check with local churches and religious organizations to see if they have programs in this area, including ESL or immigration classes and legal assistance with immigration cases.

14. THE PATIENT

It was another long day at the Louis A. Johnson VA hospital. The hours dragged by for those who lived inside the massive stone walls of the facility. It wasn't that they were poorly cared for, but they had to stay there unless someone with a pass to take them offsite showed up. For some of the patients, that was very rare as their friends and family either lived too far away or rarely visited.

Harry Jones spent the day putting together a 1500-piece puzzle of a mountain stream. It went together rapidly, since it was the fifth time it had rotated through while he was there. His memory was fine, to the point he had the color gradations memorized across the frame. The only challenging part of the process was finding where the pieces fell when someone lost in thought or zoned out from medications bumped against the table as they walked by.

He finally put the last piece in place, in the middle of the beaver dam beside the large oak tree. He sighed with satisfaction, then headed to his room for the night. There was no rush to start the next one since it would be waiting for him in the morning. His eyes were starting to ache a little from the strain of the fading light as the sun sank behind the hills behind the dog park.

Harry limped slightly as he walked back to his room, a nagging reminder of shrapnel he had taken back in Vietnam a few days before he was scheduled to come home. The fighting had been stressful enough, but the day he was injured was more intense than ever. The constant bombing and sniper fire had everyone on edge, and not many made it out alive that day. Even though he made it back to his family, he would never consider himself to be lucky for doing it. If anything, he would have rather died fighting beside his friends than to suffer years of pain punctuated by flashbacks to that fateful day he could never quite shake and the friends he lost that day.

As Harry brushed his teeth, the nurse came in with the med cart. His roommate Dean had lost an arm and a leg in the war and could barely get out of bed anymore because of his scars. By the time all of Dean's meds were pulled out, there were three pill cups waiting for him to take. It took almost as much time to rearrange the bed so he could swallow them without choking-on a good night, at least. He could only swallow one or two at a time, so Harry had finished his routine and was waiting by the sink for his round by the time Dean finished.

He had heard a faint rumble of thunder while he brushed his teeth. It had been a hot, dry week and even the overwatered lawn outside his window was starting to show stress. Harry used to enjoy running outside and playing in the rain when he was younger, making tiny irrigation ditches in the flower beds to catch the rain before it ran down the hill in front of their house to the creek. He would like to go outside in the rain tonight, but they would never let him leave the unit this late.

It was Harry's turn at the med cart. His pile of pills was small, but potent. He hated taking them, but the only chance he had of getting a good night's sleep these days was from the Schedule II drugs which eased the pain and blocked his nightmares. They worked most of the time, but still not consistently enough for him to leave the hospital. He swallowed them with a glass of water, then climbed into bed to see what would happen.

The nurse clicked off the lights as she left, but the walls still glowed from the parking lot lights outside. They gave everything an orange-tinged aura, including the displays and pictures on the wall. Looking in the mirror after the lights were off at night wasn't a good idea, since the glow behind his head reminded him of the night napalm runs in Vietnam. Not a good reminder, and one that could bring the nightmares back.

One picture he had asked to be moved so he could see it from his bed. It was a quiet country scene, one that reminded him of the farm he grew up on, down the road in Wheeling. It was of a simple ranch style house with a long front porch. Trees and flowers bloomed in front of the house, and a dirt path led to a machine shed beside it. One of the bay doors was open, with the farmer sharpening something on a grinder on a workbench.

Harry let his mind wander back to his younger days as he looked at the painting. The scraggly generic bushes beside the painted house became the stately wisteria and honeysuckle bushes where he grew up. He remembered where every tulip, daffodil and rose was in front of the house. As he thought about how his Mom had pruned the bushes to grow taller, he heard the thunder from the growing storm move down the valley into town. He remembered how some of the flowers would put off more scent after a major rain, and how it contrasted with the smell of fresh-cut hay from their pasture of native hay across the road.

After a few minutes he could feel the meds taking over. One pill made his brain a little fuzzy to disrupt his mind enough so he could sleep. Another progressively relaxed his muscles to prevent them from twitching into flight mode so quickly. Working together they helped him relax and fall asleep. His eyes were getting fuzzy, his breathing slowed, and he was close to sleep. Most of the picture faded from sight except for the farmer, who was illuminated by sparks flying off the grinding wheel.

Just then lightning struck the hill in front of his window. The glare from the bolts seared the image of the farmer into his mind, and he was back in Vietnam under fire. An involuntary scream escaped his lips, and his muscles twitched as they fought to run. The scream and rattling of his bed woke Dean, who immediately pushed the call button.

When the nurse arrived, Harry was writhing on his bed. He lunged towards the edge, trying to slide off the bed to find cover. The nurse called his name several times, but he was too far into his nightmare to recognize her. Based on previous episodes, the nurse called the doctor to get approval to start his emergency protocol. Soon his arms and legs were restrained to his bedrails, and higher doses of his anti-psychotic drugs administered. All the staff could do was monitor him and try to prevent him from hurting himself.

Harry was back in Vietnam on that fateful day that they walked into an ambush. As the firefight started, they radioed for reinforcements, but a couple bombers were the only resources that weren't committed to the fight already. The firefight was focused and intense, and most of the unit was down by the time napalm hit the hill behind their attackers. Within minutes the handful of survivors were disarmed and forced to march to the prison camp they had spent days searching for.

Most of the captives were forced into an empty bunker surrounded by razor wire. As the highest-ranking officer of the group, Harry was taken to the long, low building that looked like a machine shed sitting a few yards from the camp's headquarters. After an hour of being questioned, with the obligatory encouragement from a bamboo cane across his back and legs, they decided to up the ante. They stripped off his shirt and pants and tied him face down to a table.

The interrogator took a black bag out of a drawer near the sink. He unzipped it and removed a knife with a long, curved blade. He turned on a small motor with a grinding wheel on the bench under the window. With slow, practiced strokes he sharpened the knife, anticipating extracting answers from his latest victim. The screech of metal against stone only increased the anguish Harry felt as he waited to see what would come next.

Determination to remain calm overruled by instinct, Harry's breath rasped between his teeth through clenched lips. The ragged bursts accentuated the dryness in his mouth, aggravating his thirst caused by sweating from his fruitless attempts to flee. His muscles twitched violently, but the ties on his hands and legs remained stubbornly tied to the rough boards of the table. His muscles continued fighting for release, even as his mind resigned itself to his fate.

Harry glanced through the window, focusing on the flash

of renewed gunfire barely visible through the grimy window of the torture shack. Once again he was yanked back inside by the screech of iron on the grist stone as the soldier held the knife's blade against it, honing it into the thinnest possible edge. Each long, slow, practiced stroke sucked a little more hope from Harry's psyche. He was tied down in a way that exposed about everything, and a blade that size and shape could inflict a lot of pain in a short amount of time. As his mind began to wander ahead to the torture in store, he forced his eyes back to the flashes of bombs exploding on the horizon.

As the soldier checked the blade with his fingers, the sounds of the night flooded his ears. Crickets chirped outside the wall, accompanied by the songs of a few remaining cicadas. A dog barked as he chased a rabbit across the lawn of the house. Somewhere close by an owl hooted as darkness embraced the land. He began thinking of growing up on the farm, when things were peaceful, and all was right in the world.

A new screech jerked his attention back to the soldier. In place of the knife he now sharpened some long, thin files made for long and painful penetration. The quietness of the soldier's breathing as the hot flecks of metal shot onto his leather gloves contrasted sharply with his own panicked breathing. The strokes were faster now that the soldier didn't have to concern himself with the curve of the knife's blade, and the increasing tempo somehow edged up Harry's already racing pulse. Whatever damage done with these would be fast and vicious.

Something about this new sound drove him over the edge into panic. Maybe it was the pitch, or the overtones grating against his eardrums like explosions from missiles exploding outside, or just the sudden deviation from the routine. The what and why was unimportant. The only reality was the pulsating waves of terror washing over his body, completely paralyzing every muscle as sweat poured off his body and puddled under him. The end was near. The only questions remaining were what kind of torture he would be forced to endure, and how long it would take until it was over.

His muscles contracted against the ropes again, and his neck arched downward. It raised his head enough to see further out the window. On the edge of the clearing he saw two bursts of gunfire. The guards watching his torture grabbed their SKS carbines and headed outside. Even the soldier preparing to torture him dropped his tools, trading them for his rifle. Something was definitely going on outside the compound.

His muscles eased from exhaustion, and his head lay flat against the table once again. This didn't affect his hearing, however. The gunfire was familiar, the M1 and M16's his own unit carried. The shots came from two locations, indicating a large squad was involved in the attack. They methodically moved closer, focusing on eliminating the enemy and capturing the camp headquarters to recover whatever intelligence they could find. Protecting the prisoners was also a priority, but one best accomplished by eliminating the highest-ranking officers first.

Two bullets whizzed through the windows of the compound close to Harry. His tormentor went down quickly, so focused on the firefight in front of him that he had lost track of the action coming up from the other side. Another five minutes of intense fire directed at the main building beside the shed and silence broke out over the camp. The enemy was either dead or captured, and the conquerors made quick work of releasing the prisoners. Harry was released when they cleared the buildings, and he limped outside to join the rest of those released.

There were thirteen Marines involved in the search and destroy mission that rescued them. Some of them stood guard while waiting for the transports who would take them to safety. Two made the rounds of the prisoners, writing down who they were and anyone they knew that didn't make it long enough to be freed. They called the squad leader Jesus, and he spent time talking to each person they rescued as the recovery was coordinated.

By the time Jesus worked his way over to where he sat on a bench, Harry had time to put on his uniform and straighten it.

He used his fingers to comb his hair enough to hopefully be presentable, and splashed water on his face to clean off some of the dirt from the forced march and gritty shed. He saluted his rescuer, and they started chatting.

"Sergeant Jones," Jesus said, "What brought you to this neck of the woods?"

"Just wandered into the wrong spot about five clicks from the camp, I guess," Harry replied. "Happened yesterday on our last patrol."

"Well, don't be too hard on yourself," Jesus sympathized. "If it wasn't for you, we wouldn't have found this camp. We found the trail a couple of hours after they hit you and followed them here."

"I'm glad it was good for something. We lost a lot of good men back there," Harry winced. "I wish we could have saved more."

"We all do," Jesus agreed. "Now it is time to worry about those who are left."

With that, Jesus looked at the welts Harry had received during his interrogation. As he ran his hands along the lines on his neck and arms, the pain seemed to fade away. The blisters on his feet stopped throbbing, and the aching in his legs eased as well.

"That should feel better," Jesus said. "Just a couple more spots and you should be ready to move on."

He rested his hand over Harry's heart, and the pain from losing his friends eased. Then Jesus rested his hand on Harry's head. As it laid there, the terror and anxiety flowed out from his mind. The overwhelming terror of helplessness in the face of the unknown faded. After a few seconds Harry's mind experienced complete peace for the first time since he started fighting in the war. He closed his eyes as rest overtook him, thankful to this stranger that had rescued him in more ways than one.

"Rest well, my friend," Jesus told him.

Harry heard the footsteps of Jesus as he went on to the next former prisoner. The next footsteps he heard were different, the soft shuffle of rubber against linoleum. He stretched his arms a little and heard the clink of leather restraints against the metal rails.

Harry opened his eyes and looked up at the doctor leaning against the side of his bed in the hospital.

"Quite a ride again tonight, Harry," the doctor said. "I was hoping we were finally over those episodes."

Harry grinned up at him. "Well doctor, after tonight I don't think you will have to worry about me anymore." He closed his eyes once again and immediately sank into a deep sleep for the first time in months.

Reflections

Acts 5:16 Crowds gathered also from the towns around Jerusalem, bringing their sick and those tormented by impure spirits, and all of them were healed.

Post-Traumatic Stress Disorder (PTSD) is a relatively common condition developed by people who have experienced combat. When I say combat, I don't just mean war conditions, either. It is an extremely common side effect with victims of domestic violence and severe assault as well. While all of these result in nightmares and affects how the victim experiences life and makes decisions, the PTSD experienced by veterans from extended combat tours can prevent them from successfully returning to civilian life when their tour ends.

While this story focuses on PTSD, there are thousands of veterans in VA hospitals and extended care facilities due to injury or age-related diseases as well. As with any extended care facilities, some of these rarely have visitors and are forced to deal with the added depression of being unwanted or neglected by family and friends. Close friendships do develop between residents of these facilities but going weeks or months without seeing their own relatives takes a mental toll.

Questions for Contemplation

1. How many long-term facilities are there in your community?

2. How many veterans' organizations are there in your area? Have you ever interacted with any of them?

3. PTSD was ignored as a legitimate condition until fairly recently. This caused many people who had it to suppress theirs and deal with it as they could. For many this included isolation, drugs and violence. How can you approach older veterans who still suffer from PTSD and help them understand they are accepted and there are ways to deal with it now?

4. Veterans groups are fairly well accepted and funded, partially because there are so many of them and their numbers keep increasing. What are some ways you can become involved with them, even if you did not serve in the military yourself?

5. PTSD and other trauma-related mental health conditions can be treated with medication as well as counseling. How important is the role of personal involvement by family and friends providing support for

someone suffering from these conditions?

Call to Action

It is important to anyone who is isolated either by personal choice or by health conditions to have frequent face-to-face support from those they know. This isn't easy when their family lives hundreds of miles away, but it is important for them to make it a priority to see them as frequently as possible. Spending a day in a VA long-term care facility may not be the most exciting vacation activity you can think of, so plan ahead to take them out to dinner or shopping while you are there if they can.

There are some Christian ministries to veterans available to get ideas and support from. One is Combat Veterans Christian Ministries associated with the Wounded Warriors Project. Campus Crusade for Christ has a specific outreach for people with PTSD called American Combat Victims Need You that has videos and booklets available on how to reach out to them. New Creation Ministry has an outreach for women to help them deal with PTSD. If you are suffering from PTSD please reach out to one of these outreaches or contact a Christian counseling program in your area to see what options they have to help you.

15. FOLSOM STREET FAIR

The exhibits had closed over an hour ago, but Folsom Street still throbbed with activity. The bondage exhibitions were officially being torn down, but exhibitors were still pushing their wares to the mass of leather-clad participants walking or being led past them. Some cash changed hands, but everyone was on a mission to reach their post-event parties. The majority was headed to the Deviant party but private parties, sponsored by exhibitors for major buyers, surrounded the event. Those who didn't have an invitation to something headed to the two street stages screaming techno music.

Not everyone was looking forward to several more hours of debauchery, however. Thomas slumped in front of The Bloodhound, a country bar where his dominant had dragged him, despite his aversion to that style of music. Hands cuffed to his sides, head pulled back by the chain attached to his waist and threatened with an impatient whip, Angel had forced him out to the booths and made sure he was used as an example at several demonstrations until he was exhausted. Sure, at first it was fun and exciting, but everyone has their limits and his had been reached by the middle of the afternoon.

The day had opened his eyes in more ways than one. There were layers of sexual excitement and torture far beyond his imagination. Even though toys in the booths were mostly redundant, the ways they could be used to bring pleasure or humiliation varied dramatically as they traveled into the darker corners of the fair. Enjoyment had its limits in many respects. The one thing that seemed to be limitless is the power one person could wield or have taken from them.

The one thing Thomas had learned that afternoon was

Angel's true nature. He had considered himself lucky when Angel invited him to the fair, especially considering the number of sycophants who begged for his attention at every bar and event. In reality, he was the newest and most inexperienced in the fringe of Angel's circle, and the thought of physically and mentally destroying the will of a newcomer was far more exiting to Angel than any sexual release he could imagine.

Angel headed into the bar for drinks with some of his inner circle, but Thomas would not be a part of that group. In another show of unfeeling domination, Angel tied him to the hitching post outside. Alone in the middle of the crowd of revelers, he was at last able to get some rest. Despite his hunger and thirst, he finally had a chance to rest from the S&M marathon he had been running. He closed his eyes and leaned against the post, trying to get some sleep before the nightmare resumed.

Despite the pain and exhaustion Thomas felt, his mind remained clear. This new thing was nothing he wanted a part of. He would escape the first chance he had, but the cuffs and chains kept him tied to Angel just as his search for fulfillment tied him to a never-ending list of things he had experimented with. His intellectual phase left him as empty as his adventure phase, and this sexual phase was sucking him further into the hole of emptiness and self-loathing. Whatever he was seeking would not be found in the direction he was being dragged now.

He jerked awake when a hand touched his shoulder. An involuntary shudder raced through him at the thought of what would happen next. Then again, if it had been Angel his jerk back to reality would have been a spiked cuff across the face or boot stomped into his stomach. He cautiously opened his eyes to see who had awakened him.

The person standing in front of him was dressed simply in jeans, t-shirt and tennis shoes. No wonder he hadn't heard the stomping of boots he was listening for in his stupor. Instead of ignoring or mocking him, the stranger's gentle brown eyes stared directly into his red-shot blue ones, concern radiating from his face.

"Drink this. It will help you feel better."

The stranger raised the glass to his lips so he could sip its contents. Thomas was desperately thirsty but prepared himself for something revolting. What ran into his mouth was simply water-cool, refreshing water that rinsed the dust and taste of rubber away. That's when he realized that he wasn't gagged anymore. He jerked his head away from the glass and looked down to see the chains and handcuffs laying open in the dirt in front of him. He cowered against the post again, knowing he would be whipped mercilessly by Angel when he discovered he had escaped.

"No, my friend. There will not be any more of that tonight-or ever again, if you choose. Look over there. Angel is starting to understand how you feel."

Thomas' gaze followed the direction of the stranger's finger. Angel was lying face down in the dirt, his arms down as the police put him in handcuffs and shackled his ankles. After he was restrained, they jerked him to his feet and dragged him to a police car. The door slammed on him, then disappeared into the night.

Thomas said, "I don't understand. What happened? How did you know I was his slave?"

The stranger said, "You asked God to deliver you, and I am here to answer your prayer. Just consider what is happening to Angel as a little divine retribution for his sins. Now go. Go back to the church you turned away from many years ago and you will find the answer to your inner thirst. You knew it many years ago, and now it is time to find it again."

The stranger stood up and walked down the street, a different object of ridicule in the mass of skin and leather flowing down the street. Thomas gingerly stood up, muscles still shaking from the ordeal of the day. He went to the cheap hotel where he was staying, packed his suitcase, and pulled his car out of the parking lot. Finally, he was going home.

Reflections

Leviticus 20:13 "'If a man has sexual relations with a man as one does with a woman, both of them have done what is detestable. They are to be put to death; their blood will be on their own heads.

Throughout history Christians have a habit of taking one group of individuals associated with one issue and making them their enemy of choice for several years until the movement loses steam, which causes them to move on to a new group. The target frequently represents one specific sin, which is blown up in importance by the movement to make it seem to be more significant than all the others.

This isn't necessarily new. The Israelites focused on worshipping idols on and off throughout the Old Testament. More recently in church history the "worst" sin has moved from slavery to alcohol (Prohibition) to the current focus on homosexuality. While an unbiased reader will clearly find verses in the Bible calling homosexuality a sin (Romans 1:26, 1 Timothy 1:10, Jude 1:7), it is impossible to find any text which justifies calling this sin either more or less evil than any other one.

To treat the LGBQT part of culture as unworthy of the church reaching out to them violates Christ's command to go into all parts of the earth. Like people who practice the sin of stealing, that culture ranges from those who steal pencils or pens from work to those who kill people while robbing stores or banks. All are thieves, but some practice the lifestyle more seriously than others. It doesn't matter how often they steal, or how valuable the items are they take, they are all committing sin and need Christians to show God loves and cares for them to lead them to a relationship with Jesus Christ.

Questions for Contemplation

1. What have you been taught about homosexuality in your church?

2. How have you seen Christians in your community treat those who have come out as being a member of the LBGQT community?

3. Would you ever consider treating a thief or adulterer the way you have treated someone you knew was a part of the LBGQT community? If so, how do you justify treating them differently?

4. Do you believe, or have you been taught, the gift of God's salvation and teachings that forgiveness allows you to live a life of freedom from former sins applies differently to those in the LBGQT community?

5. Does your church welcome those who have asked for forgiveness for their LBGQT lifestyles and use them in leadership positions in the same way they use people who come from backgrounds of other sins?

Call to Action

The most obvious step for reaching those in the LBGQT community is to stop treating them differently than others we believe aren't following God's will. You can't catch homosexuality from them any more than you can catch lung cancer from a smoker. Pretending their attraction to someone of the same sex will automatically disappear once they accept Christ as their savior is as naïve as expecting your urge to look at porn will just disappear if you pray hard enough. Yes, it does happen with some people, but for most it is an ongoing struggle that is made much easier by having accountability partners and trained counselors to lead them through the process.

There are many groups out there who believe someone who has acted on their inclinations of homosexuality can be cured through castration or chemical or electrical treatments. The truth is the only cure that exists is the grace of God aided by the loving support of true Christians.

It is difficult to sort out groups who use excessive and un-scientific methods to force conversion from this lifestyle, but here are a couple that seem to be legitimate. The first group is Exodus International of North America. The second group is called Homosexuals Anonymous. If you wish to learn how to reach out effectively to those in the LBGQT community around you, or if you are struggling with these urges yourself, please contact them for more information.

16. THE INCIDENT

It was another warm summer day in Tennessee. The sun was just peaking over the mountains when Harrison left for work, too tired from its last spin around the world to pull itself over the jagged peak without resting a bit. Heavy dew and mist from the stream by his house covered his car, so he turned on the windshield wipers and defroster to clear a spot big enough to see through until the sun gathered enough courage to dry the extra moisture out of the air.

When Harrison cleared the driveway, his focus shifted towards work. Another day of shifting papers around while waiting for the next experiment to clear the administrative hurdles and the rest of the supplies to come in. At least there was always some paperwork to shuffle to keep the pencil pushers happy and occupied.

His wife Sarah and stepdaughter Hailey hadn't moved a muscle when as he left. School was out and his wife only worked four days a week so they had stayed up late and wouldn't wake up until around eleven. He often wondered what it would be like to have three days a week to work on projects around the house instead of two, but it seemed every time he took an extra day off, he was either sick or it rained so he didn't get anything done.

He sighed as he thought of his wife. She had been avoiding him for months, always finding an excuse to be gone instead of spending time with him or doing things around the house. She had grown more demanding, insisting on knowing everything he did and everywhere he went, while avoiding telling him anything she did. It was a no-win situation, one he prayed about for months without any answers other than it was an issue with her refusing to do what God was asking her.

The last three or four days had been slightly different. Sarah had actually been home at night when it was time to go to bed, so he was starting to have some hope. Harrison was just at a loss of how to break the ice. Whenever he went to bed, she was busy doing homework, and he had been yelled at too many times for interrupting someone studying to know what to say or if it would be worth the effort. It was an issue his mind turned to frequently as he was trying to focus on his work that day.

Driving home that night, Harrison started to get excited. If Sarah was really making an effort to straighten things out, maybe she would be waiting for him at the house with something cooking for dinner like she used to do when they were first married. Maybe she stayed home and mowed the lawn which was getting long since it had rained for several days and had been too muddy for him to do it. Maybe they would finally make up and she would tell him what had been bothering her.

The anticipation quickly faded when he pulled up to the house. Her car was nowhere to be seen, so she had disappeared again and it was hard to tell when she would show up. Instead of being greeted with a hug and a kiss and the smell of something good cooking it looked like it would be another night of scrounging something from the fridge.

The grass hadn't been touched, but she had been busy. Sarah's ex-husband was the caretaker at a cemetery, and she had become convinced her lawn needed mowed once a week without anything out of place. Then again, she was all about appearances and looking good on the outside. She had pulled all the protective fences from around the trees he had planted, leaving them vulnerable to the deer grazing in the yard. The weeds around the trees hadn't been touched, but the fencing was piled at the back of the yard. What was left of the hay bales from an ongoing landscaping project had disappeared, just as she had threatened even though she knew he worked on them every day the weather allowed.

That was the straw that broke the camel's back. Harrison

went into the kitchen to find something to eat, pondering how many times Sarah had done things that affected the rest of the family without discussing it with him or considering the consequences. As he pulled some salmon out of the freezer to thaw, a thought came into his head. Since she obviously didn't listen or care about doing things that affected him without talking about them first, it was time for her to have the same experience.

He went into the bedroom to change into his work clothes. Even though Sarah had pulled her control crap and disappearing act again, the lawn still needed mowed so he would work on that. The landscaping would have to wait. On the way out to the shed to get the lawnmower he picked up two of her favorite appliances, one for each bale of hay that disappeared, and tucked them into protected spots in the shed. Two can play this game, and it was far past time for her to taste her own medicine.

He prepped the mower and started it. This was not as easy as it should have been, especially since it was brand new. The odd sound and vibration when it ran indicated something major was wrong. Oh well, there wasn't time to have it looked at and no money in the budget to buy a second mower that month so it would have to do.

The first round was always the most difficult, since part of the yard was a pile of buried trees covered with weeds and impossible to mow with the steep banks and large rocks. The trick was to get as close to the stumps and rocks as possible without hitting anything. From the short track of mowed grass it was obvious Sarah had started to mow, and the first place she went for was the weeds he had told her at least three times were too rough to mow. The cut grass ended where a brick stuck out of the ground, so he knew how the new mower had been damaged. The noise was getting worse, especially when going down the bank towards the creek.

Just then Sara pulled in the driveway. She got out of the car and went into the house without acknowledging Harrison, which was typical. Apparently she was planning on cooking for the first time in several days, because within minutes she yanked the door open and started yelling at him. It took a few minutes for him to hear her over the rattle of the lawn mower and babbling of the brook.

"Harrison," Sarah yelled again. "Where's my Hot Pot?"

Harrison was feeling slightly more positive about the situation. He had just found one of the hay bales rolled down the hill, but at least she hadn't conned someone into taking it away like she had threatened. Unfortunately, the damaged lawn mower did not let his mood improve much, so she wasn't going to get off the hook easily. "It's in the shed," he replied.

Her answer was predictable; "Go get it." Even though she had spent part of her day rearranging the yard without discussing it with him, she still expected him to drop everything and do her bidding as soon as she snapped her fingers. Not that he was the only one she treated that way. She did the same to her family and co-workers as well-then complained about how insensitive and uncaring they were to her.

"No. Go find it yourself," he yelled back. It was her turn to play the guessing game of where-did-my-stuff-disappear-to-this-time. Hopefully this would wake her up to how inconsiderate and insensitive her thoughts and actions were, but he had little hope since she had gotten away with this for decades. Everyone else was either too scared to stand up to her or, as in previous marriages, just ignored her until her narcissism led her to find someone else who caved to her demands-at least temporarily.

"You go get it!" Sarah demanded.

"No, go find it yourself," he yelled again.

She kept screaming her demands. Soon she was stamping her feet and shaking her fist, which was typical of one of her tantrums when she didn't get her way. By this time the neighbors across the road were listening to the fracas, shaking their heads from their front porch, which she could not see.

Harrison was in the middle of a particularly tricky part of the creek bank, and just ignored her escalating fury. She finally slammed the door, went out to the shed and did a cursory glance. When she found the first appliance, she stomped back into the house with it, then opened the door and started yelling at him again.

He continued to ignore her, fighting with the bank and mower which was starting to cut out now. Sarah's temper tantrum would have been embarrassing for a two-year-old. It was outright humiliating for someone her age to be throwing, especially where the neighbors could see. When she finally realized her show wasn't going to change anything, she slammed the door once again and went back to the shed.

After a few minutes she went back to the house. He wondered why she didn't have the other appliance, since it was right beside the first one. Good, Harrison thought. Hopefully the show is over, and she will have learned something from it.

That was wishful thinking on his part, unfortunately. In a few seconds the door burst open again and Sara headed straight towards Harrison. He was working on another steep part of the bank, which was still slick from the rain earlier that day. Between the cut grass and the rain it took all of his concentration to keep his footing and not lose the mower into the creek. He continued mowing the slope, working his way across the edge until Sarah blocked his way.

As soon as she got close, Sarah started screaming at him again. Nothing new, just repeating what she had screamed from the doorway. Harrison kept the mower running, afraid it wouldn't start again if he let go of the handle. That didn't stop her. In fact, she grabbed the mower and yanked it out of his hands. Fortunately he was able to get one hand on it enough to keep it from going into the creek, but it was close.

The screaming went on for over five minutes. She yelled so fast it seemed she didn't take a breath, and the words ran together so it was impossible to understand what she was saying. Halfway through her tirade she picked up a rock by her foot and threw it at him. It hit him on the shoulder and deflected into his chest, leaving a small bruise. She had yelled and screamed and thrown things at him before, but this tantrum had reached a dangerous level.

Apparently throwing the rock wasn't enough. She moved into him, pressing her body into his, and began thrusting against him, trying to knock him off balance. She shoved her face into his until her nose flattened against his. She finally slowed down talking enough so he could finally understand her. It wasn't an easing of the tantrum, though. It was an acceleration: with each word she pounded her nose into his face, trying to force him backwards onto the ground.

At this point Hailey emerged from the house far enough to watch the show. It was a scene she had obviously watched before, but with Sarah's ex-husband. She stood there smirking, waiting for Harrison to cave like Sarah's previous husband had. Physical intimidation and screaming to get what they wanted was obviously ingrained in their previous family, because Hailey had used the tactics on more than one occasion in the last year herself.

"WHERE. IS. MY. HOT. POT," Sarah thumped into his face.

"In the shed, right by the other one," Harrison replied.

"GO GET IT," she pounded back.

"I'm busy. You know where it is, so get it yourself," he replied.

"WHY DID YOU DO IT," she demanded. "YOU DIDN'T HAVE ANY RIGHT."

"And you didn't have any right to move the hay bales and fencing," he said.

That set her off again. It was back to screaming at full volume and speed because, like with everything else, nothing could be her fault. She didn't stop to breathe, just a constant barrage of words and vulgarity. She was putting more and more force against him, and it was clear there wasn't any stopping her. Apparently not happy that she was not getting her point across, she punched him with her left hand, hitting the brim of his cap and deflecting into his nose. It partially knocked his glasses off, which he quickly adjusted.

Harrison couldn't take any more of it. He put one hand on each shoulder and slowly moved her away until he had enough room to protect himself.. When she had taken two steps backwards he released her shoulders and turned back to the mower. She stopped screaming briefly, then changed her tune.

"Abuser! Wife beater," Sarah screamed.

"Abuser," was quickly echoed from the porch by Hailey. The trained parrot was in full cry, echoing whatever her mother said.

By some miracle the mower started again, and Harrison continued mowing. As he mowed, he thought about what had happened. Sarah had crossed the line, again, and gone way too far. Combined with what she was yelling at the end, she was obviously going to pull something. He had come to realize she lied far more often than she told the truth, especially when manipulating people to get her way. She was going to not only cover up what she had done, with her daughter a willing conspirator, but she was going to lie to her parents to shift all the blame on him. Again.

The motor soon gave a death rattle and rasped into silence. He tried starting it again, but the motor was frozen. He sighed and pushed it back to the shed. When he got there, he saw Sarah had thrown most of his tools out of the door. That further proved what he had to do. He pulled out his phone and called the sheriff. Obviously, nobody else had stood up to Sarah when she had acted like that, but her time had come. He reported the incident, then waited for a deputy to come and remove her from the property to give her time to reflect on the seriousness of what she had done.

When he got to the front of the house, Sarah was loading stuff into the car. Good. The rest should be easy. She had called in her usual minions when she was causing trouble, so he went and sat on a stump waiting for the sheriff. As he sat there, a lone man walked down the road and over towards him. Kind of strange that far into the country, but he hadn't meant anyone that wasn't a new friend yet.

"Rough night, huh," asked the stranger?

"You could say that. Thought it was going to be a good one, then all hell broke loose," Harrison said.

"I wouldn't quite go that far, but I'm sure it seems that way," said the stranger. "I'm Jesus, and my friends and I were just checking out the scenery when we heard the commotion."

"She does have a good set of lungs on her," Harrison said. "That's one of her few good assets."

Jesus said, "Well, actually she is quite a force of good when she does what she knows she should do. That just hasn't happened very often since she was a teenager."

"She was very impressive when I knew her growing up," Harrison agreed. "Now it seems like she works hard to do everything the opposite of how she lived then but makes a big show about being the same person in front of her parents.:

"By this time even her parents have begun to suspect," Jesus stated. "When you live two different lives so opposite of each other it's difficult to keep your lies straight all of the time.

Just then the sheriff pulled into the driveway and headed into the house. Might as well let her put on her show first. If he had any experience it won't take him long to figure out the truth.

"Well, looks like the show is about to start," Jesus said. "I'll let you gather your thoughts. It's going to be a long, rough haul for you, but if you keep doing what you know is right things will work out in the end.

With that Jesus went back to the road and disappeared into the night. Harrison went over what had happened in his mind again, still in shock at what had occurred. He breathed a quick prayer for truth and wisdom for the sheriff when he started heading his way. This was not the future he moved here for, and he hoped this would finally wake Sarah up.

Reflections

Ephesians 5:33 However, each of you also must love your wife as he loves himself, and the wife must respect her husband.

Domestic violence is a topic the church generally doesn't want to deal with. When someone approaches a church leader about it, the typical response is denial because the person accused is such a good Christian or leader or whatever. The culture of denial allows the abuse to continue indefinitely, without any intervention or consequences to the perpetrator.

When someone does pay attention to the victim, they are generally told to stay with the abuser and pray for them. This response just covers up the problem and allows anyone aware of the situation to wash their hands of responsibility with the same success as Ceaser when he washed his hands after sentencing Jesus to death. It is important to pray for the abuser, but unless there are consequences including pulling the victim out of the situation and confrontation about the situation nothing will change.

It is important to be cautious when accusations of abuse are made, however. In today's culture a simple accusation to the police or child services is essentially a guilty sentence until proven innocent. In the case of actual abuse this is a good thing, but when someone is out for revenge or trying to get an edge in a custody battle this is a common tactic which has harmed thousands of innocent spouses. That is why it is important to get a professional counselor involved, to not only determine if the accusation is true but to unleash a stream of resources to help those who are truly victims.

Domestic violence occurs with both sexes. Men are more likely to be abusers than women, but the difference in abuse rates has decreased over the years. Most shelters and aid for abuse victims are geared towards women, and trainings focus on helping women more than men. Men have a harder time being believed when they come forward with stories of abuse, and society tends to look down on them because they are supposed to be "tough" and "take it" while women are treated as the weaker sex in need of protection. This is at the least sexist and contributes to the culture of allowing female abusers to continue their behaviors while aggressively pursuing any hints of abuse from males.

Questions for Contemplation

1. Are there any organizations in your community to help victims of domestic abuse? If so, are their services focused on temporary shelter or do they offer ongoing assistance to help victims recover from the situation?

2. Have you ever heard of a domestic abuse situation in your church? If so, how did the church leaders handle the situation?

3. Everyone gets angry at times, and there are many legitimate reasons to do so. Domestic violence is a consistent pattern of one person blaming their significant other for everything and using intimidation and violence to control them. What are signs to look for to determine if a situation has escalated from simple frustration to a domestic violence situation?

4. Narcissists have a higher rate of abuse than other personality types. This happens because they not only rationalize their behavior to excuse it, but they never take responsibility for their own actions-no matter how horrific they become. Even if they apologize after an episode, they do not believe they did anything wrong and only use it as a ploy to manipulate their victim into staying. Do you know anyone who fits this pattern of behavior?

5. Abusers will never change their behaviors until they are genuinely convinced what they are doing is wrong. Sometimes this happens when the victims leave. It is more likely to occur after they are arrested for physical violence. Church leaders can attempt to convince someone they are not acting right by consistently confronting the behavior and providing ongoing professional therapy to help them change their thinking and acting patterns. What resources in your local church or other Christian organizations in your community are equipped to intervene in a domestic violence situation?

Call to Action

The first step to stopping domestic violence is to learn the signs of when it is happening. Many organizations who assist domestic violence victims have community training events to not only recognize these situations but know what to do to help victims get help, including providing temporary shelter- at least for women. If someone comes to you about a domestic violence situation, listen to them and suggest alternatives, but understand the victim typically is convinced they are worthless and deserve the abuse so they are highly reluctant to take the first steps to escape it.

It is also extremely important for every one of both sexes to take an honest look at their own thoughts and behaviors. If you believe other people are to blame for your shortcomings and have frequent outbursts of anger, you are either at the edge or have crossed the line into abuse yourself and need to immediately get help. If you initiate any physical violence-pushing, shoving, slapping, throwing things or hitting-you are guilty of domestic violence and need to get help immediately. You are out of control. It isn't funny or cute or excusable, no matter what sex you are. Get help and stop your abuse today.

If you are a domestic violence victim whose life is in danger, you can find a shelter who will help remove you from your situation at domesticshelters.org. SAFE in a national organization who staffs the National Domestic Violence Hotline at 1-855-662-SAFE and local shelters but focus more on women and can be biased against re-ligious groups. Focus Ministries is Christian based and geared towards women and families. Ministry Matters is associated with Chuck Coulson and part of his ministry focuses on domestic abuse. If you are or think you may be a victim of domestic abuse and your local church is unwilling to help, contact one of these ministries to see if they have can refer you to an organization in your area who can help you.

17. THE SUN DANCE

Wisps of sand driven by the wind curled along the barren Arizona desert, twisting illusions of spirits hovering over the landscape. Stubby prickly pear stubbornly endured the predawn chill. The animals who called this patch of seared earth home hid in burrows or under the spiny cactus spines, settling down to sleep as the darkness protecting them as they hunted faded. This time of day was usually marked by silence, broken only by an occasional puff of wind, but today was not a typical day.

A wooden pole towered out of the sand. Weathered by the sun and blasted by sandstorms, it had been carried to this sacred place of desolation decades ago from the mountains where the elders were put to rest. Although time and exposure were having their effects, it still stood proudly in the center of this desolation.

Spaced evenly around the center pole were twelve smaller poles, all tied into the base. Interwoven circles among circles, a grand pattern representing the harmony of the Great Spirit, Earth, the Animals and Man. Long ropes hung limply in pairs from the tops of the poles, anchored to the sand by the bits of bone and sticks attached to leather thongs at the ends of each one. Dried blood tinged the ends of most of the thongs, but here and there a few new ones replaced those ruined by time and weather.

East of the poles, preparations were in full swing. Flames danced in the air under grills that would soon be covered with venison, goat and large pots of stew. Tables and chairs rolled out of dusty pickups, following passengers out of their beds when they arrived. The Singer weaved his way to the sweat lodge at the edge of the camp and around the poles, chanting prayers to purify the grounds before the festivities began in earnest.

As dawn began lighting the eastern edge of the sky, three young braves left the sweat lodge and came towards the poles. They had laid on their backs in the sweat lodge, eyes closed, as the combination of hallucinogenic mushrooms and intense meditation numbed their awareness of the external. The Singer pushed sharpened bones through each side of the upper abs of each brave, who barely twitched in their enhanced state. When the first light of dawn hit the top of the mesa on the west side of the valley, the Singer led them to the east side of a smaller pole and tied the ends of each bone to the ropes with deer sinew.

The drums began beating as sunlight oozed onto the far side of the valley. The Hatali began his ritual dance around the braves, placing a stick with a feather in the mouth of each. With everything in place and the edge of the sun wedging above the east ridge, the braves leaned away from the pole and began shuffling their feet as the Sun Dance began. Their test of endurance began in a religious and drug-induced haze. Smoke from the cooking fires mixed with the wisps rising off the desert floor to form surreal visions of glistening bodies of their ancestors being chased by a White Buffalo as the sun heaved itself into the sky.

The crowd grew as the morning chills were chased from the desert sands as the sun crested the eastern ridge. More First Americans drove across the trackless wasteland towards the sacred spot with people balancing more food for the long day of ceremony and feasting in their laps. A few traditionalists could be seen walking through the cacti, dark dots inching through the sea of sand.

As the sun rose higher, heat waves started dancing off the hard-packed sand below the brave's feet. They slowly moved their positions around their poles to stay facing the sun as it arched across the sky. Periodic breaks for drinks and more peyote kept the young men focused and determined, with occasional hallucinations twistimg through their bodies. When the braves reached the point of exhaustion they began to sag against the ropes, causing the bones in their chests to lift their pectoral muscles away from their ribs. The sharp pain quickly penetrated their mental fog and restarted their dancing feet to ease their pain.

The observers settled in under teepees and canopies for relief from the heat. When preparations for lunch were finished, a line formed by the tables. Eating was light, though, out of respect for the dancers and appetites oppressed from the heat. The elders and men were served first, then the young adults and children turned the buffet area into an area for playing and flirting. Everyone took their turn showing respect by greeting and listening to the tribal chiefs and elders before rushing off to their own pursuits.

When the meal ended, the fires were re-stoked and new pots hung over them for cooking the stews and breads for the evening meal. Old mixed with the new as coolers surrounded the campfires. As food for supper began to give off their aromas, the lines to the buffet area swelled again to use the leftovers as weapons against hunger pangs.

The intensity of the dancers waxed and waned through the day. When they began to slow down, the Singer would weave his way behind the trio, chanting prayers to the Great Spirit to inspire them as the drums intensified. When the dancers were reinvigorated, the Singer rested in the shade and someone else would begin singing traditional songs of inspiration. The elders and children could be seen resting their eyes in the early afternoon, preparing for a long night of feasting and celebration.

As the shadows began creeping across the valley floor, a group of thirteen men crested the mountain behind the celebration. As the strangers came near, they were met by several members of the tribe who discouraged them from coming to the sacred ritual. With a little persuasion the group was allowed to enter the tents to refresh themselves but were forbidden to enter the sacred circle where the dance was taking place. They settled into a far corner of one of the tents with a little food and drink, where they were kept under a cautious eye.

Tantalizing smells from the cooking fires intensified as it neared dark. As the sun began sinking on the far side of the valley, the drums beat more intensely, and the Singer's chanting increased in volume. The dancers picked up their pace, sensing the end was approaching. The spectators circled around the path of pulverized sand, whooping and shouting encouragement to the dancers so close to reaching their goal.

When the sun slid down the far side of the slope and drug the last of its direct light from the valley, the drums and chanting halted abruptly. The Singer approached each brave and untied their thongs, then led them back to the sweat lodge where he removed the bones from their chest. The dance was officially over, and they were allowed some time to recover.

There was a flurry of activity outside. The large bonfire the men had built during the day was lit as the women finished preparing the evening feast. The drummers rested before their services were needed again. More people came to join in the festivities, bringing more food and drinks. As the crowd swelled and the flow of alcohol increased, the small group was able to move more freely. Jesus quietly led them out behind the tents for some quiet and reflection.

When the newly killed deer roasting on a spit was deemed ready, two older teens carried it to the place of honor at the end of the buffet tables. The dancers were brought out of the tent, half asleep and still woozy from the peyote they had consumed. The Singer gave a prayer of blessing over the feast, and a rather long oration honoring the Sun Dance, the now men who had just finished it, and the Great Spirit in general. When he saw the dancers begin wavering from exhaustion, he wrapped it up and the dancers and Singer went through the line first. The chiefs and elders followed, with the women and children bringing up the rear. After everyone was seated, the few outsiders were allowed to fill their plates and return to their seats at the end of the tent.

The meal was full of ritual, from the order of people through the line to the presentation of choice parts to the chiefs, to the courtship roles of teenagers, to how the children interacted with each other and the elders. There was even a certain way the food was arranged on the serving tables, reflecting the honor of the roasted deer, down to the modern salads and side dishes crammed together at the far end. Even the few strangers unknowingly participated in some of the rituals, but everyone had their fill by the end with plenty left to snack on as the celebration continued.

When most people had finished eating, the Singer stood by the head table and introduced each dancer in turn, who described what he saw and felt during the ritual, including supernatural interventions and visions he could remember. The first two speakers were extremely animated, full of colorful tales. The last dancer seemed subdued in his tale, with incomplete descriptions and a halting delivery. At the end of each talk the Singer gave an interpretation of the experience and predictions for the brave's future. When all three stories were complete, the crowd followed the chiefs outside to the bonfire for the rest of the celebration.

As the flames leaped into the starlit sky, the drums began to beat once again. The Singer and other professional performers presented a powerful program about the religion and history of the tribe through songs, dances and recitations. When the program was over, the sky filled with whoops and animal calls and a community dance began. The celebration lasted far into the night, with exhausted participants wandering off to their teepees, tents and vehicles when they could no longer continue.

Not everyone went out to the bonfire, however. The oldest members of the tribe simply pulled their chairs to the edges of the tents to observe the festivities. The third brave also remained in the tent. He slowly walked down the buffet table, randomly pausing to stare deeply into the dish in front of him as if trying to find some great meaning in it. He moved forward a few steps and repeated the process until he came to the end of the buffet. Seeming to find no great revelation in any of the dishes, he moved on in a haze until he brushed against Andrew, who was sitting on the edge.

"Excuse me, sir," the brave said, "I didn't see you there."

"It's ok," replied Andrew. "I'm surprised you aren't out dancing at the bonfire. Why are you still here?"

"I'd rather be alone," he said.

"The real question is, why were you afraid to tell the story of your dance," Jesus asked?

"I don't want to talk about it," he replied.

"You are among friends here," Jesus said. "We may be strangers, but we are friends and you can tell us anything. Your friends are distracted by the dancing and the elders can't hear you over the music."

"I'm not sure about this, but I have to talk to someone," he said. "The reason I had trouble telling my story is there wasn't much to tell. I danced like the others, but all I felt was exhaustion and pain. I didn't see any visions, and nothing came to help me. It was hours of pain without anything happening. How can I feel like this when the others had amazing experiences?"

"Are you sure they had the experiences they claimed," Jesus asked? "Or were they rehearsed stories suggested by the Singer hallucinated through the peyote while they were exhausted?"

He hung his head slightly. "The Singer did suggest some things that should happen while we danced. Perhaps at least some of it was imagination. I just wish there was something more out there that could be experienced. Something greater than the calm reassurance of the Great Spirit and Earth Mother."

"There is," Jesus replied. He then talked about the Father God and how he had been sent to the earth to tell people how to have a personal relationship with him that went far beyond the constant companionship of nature.

"I understand," he said. "How do I get this relationship?"

Jesus answered, "Just believe and follow my instruc-

tions." He then gave a talk about how to love yourself and your neighbor.

"Thank you, sir," he replied. "I must go out and play my part in the festivities before I'm missed. I will not forget this."

"Go in peace," Jesus said.

The brave walked with a light step to the dancing by the bonfire. Jesus got up, and his followers went up along with him as he walked back into the desert towards the nearest town. Their mission was accomplished, so they followed the moon towards their next task.

Reflections

2 Kings 17:34 To this day they persist in their former practices. They neither worship the Lord nor adhere to the decrees and regulations, the laws and commands that the Lord gave the descendants of Jacob, whom he named Israel.

Native American cultures can't be shoved into one box, not only because of the diversity of tribes but also because of the diversity of experiences those tribes have experienced. While the tribes have been mistreated by the United States government in the past, a coordinated effort has been made to ensure they have been treated well for many years.

Many tribes were forced out of their nations into lands with different ecologies making survival difficult. Alcohol was introduced by soldiers, then Native Americans were banned from drinking it which increased its attraction, and now it plays an active role in supporting them through casino sales. Traditional roles and beliefs were outlawed, and children banned from learning them, which greatly disrupted their ethics and morals.

Having their lives completely disrupted resulted in many ongoing problems. A cultural depression has developed, which has resulted in high rates of alcoholism, drug abuse and suicide. Depressed tribal economies are rampant, with reluctance by a decreasing number to pursue careers outside of those occupations traditionally practiced. As with other cultures, the number of children who respect and practice the traditional religions has decreased.

Questions for Contemplation

1. Forcing Native American children to attend boarding schools with little to no contact with their parents was one way to force them to accept American values, including Christianity. While they may have learned more about the outside culture, it ingrained a fear and hatred of the government and outsiders. What steps can be taken now to overcome any residual distrust caused by this treatment?

2. Trying to force someone to change is always doomed to failure. Change is a choice, which may come about by being exposed to other approaches. What ways would be more effective to reach other cultures than through wars and forced indoctrination?

3. Like in New Guinea and other locations, the diversity between tribes located even short distances away makes trying to reach every tribe the same way ineffective and inefficient. How important is it to develop outreach programs with basic guidelines that can be implemented flexibly?

4. Programs have existed for many years to address alco-

holism and drug abuse among Native Americans, but user rates have not changed that significantly. What do you think are the root causes behind drug and alcohol abuse, and how would addressing them make a difference in their use?

5. There are missions on reservations all over the United States. Some of them have been very effective in becoming accepted and providing health and educational services. However, when a mission closes many of those around it mirror the rest of their culture within a few years. Why do you think this phenomenon occurs?

Call to Action

As with all cultures, treating Native Americans as equals and becoming friends with them is important. Racism of any kind does not fit the Christian model. Treating anyone as a stereotype is wrong not only in that every person is different, but also because it tends to lead them to act like the stereotype instead of having the freedom to be themselves.

Since drug and alcohol addiction is a common problem in these cultures, addressing them from a Christian perspective is a useful way to positively affect them if approached correctly. Health care in remote areas is still an issue, so addressing those needs are important. Anything ongoing ministries which address the depressed economies of the tribes are helpful.

There are many local missions who can use financial support and supplies. One is Free Trinity Navaho Mission in Gallup, New Mexico. Campus Crusade for Christ has a ministry in Montana that reaches out to the Dakotas, Crow and other tribes re-located to reservations there. The Saint Stephens Mission in the Wind River Reservation in Wyoming reaches out to the Northern Arapaho and Eastern Shoshone. Contact your local church to find out the needs of the Native American ministries they support and how to go on short-term missions to help them.

18. THE RALLY

Gene Stubbins is a relatively average man. He stands five foot seven inches tall, with a slightly muscular build and a little bubble in the middle to help him stay balanced. He has salt and pepper hair, and a beard that almost touches his chest. He has a wife, two teenagers, and works full time at an architectural firm to support them.

When there weren't any kid's activities scheduled on the weekend, Gene enjoys his hobbies. His favorite thing to do is hop on his Harley Softail Deluxe when the weather is decent. It doesn't matter if it is a quick ride through the country with his friends or going on a poker run to raise money for someone, a little road therapy helps calm his nerves and refocus on what is really important in life.

The throb of the twin exhausts on the bike helps drown out the thumping of the blueprint printers and whispered gossip by the gurgling water dispenser throughout the week. The wind whistling past his helmet eases the thump of the HVAC system trying to enforce temperature conformity throughout the office building. The blurs of the curving lines on the road helps smooth over the straight lines of the apartment building plans which keep coming back to his computer screen for endless revisions.

This ride is different, however. He snaps on his Viking saddlebags and tied his camping gear onto the luggage rack behind the sissy seat. His wife Ellen climbs on behind him and they are off to the mother of all motorcycle rallies in Sturgis, South Dakota. It would be a week immersed in motorcycle lore and legend with hundreds of Harley riders from around the country.

Even though the rally is a little bit of organized chaos, the real adventure would be getting there and back. They were going with a couple of their friends from Nicholson, Ohio and connecting with a larger group somewhere along Interstate 74. There is safety in numbers, and you never knew when being in a group with a creative mechanic would come in handy.

The ride there was relatively uneventful. Part of the way they rode through rain, which was typical. They did hide out under an overpass when a hailstorm swept over them, but it passed quickly, and the hailstones were soft pea size that didn't do any damage. Traffic was slow through Indianapolis and around Lincoln, Nebraska after they caught Interstate 80, but that was to be expected around cities at the peak of vacation season.

Before they got to Sturgis they unloaded their camping supplies in the Boulder Creek campground, a favorite and less expensive option to camps in town. The camping areas were crowded with bikers anyway, which made it highly unlikely that anyone would cause trouble for long before they were corralled by the security teams organized by various clubs. They set up their tent and unloaded most of their luggage, then headed to the rally for some entertainment and to pick up food from the Grocery Mart.

Traffic crawled with thousands of bikes crowding into town. They finally made it through Main Street and to Gold Pan Pizza, one of their favorite stops. They cleaned off a table for themselves and ordered the Supreme. It took a while to get their food, but it was a great way to refuel after the trip.

After eating, they walked through downtown to see where everything was. The sidewalks were crowded with food trucks and companies who sold everything imaginable related to bikes. The wheelie contests were in full throttle, throwing off enough tire smoke to help deter the mosquitoes thrilled with the massive food supply. Music filled the air from bars and vendor booths, so if you didn't like what you heard in one spot you could walk ten steps and listen to something different.

They headed back to camp early that night to rest up from their trip. Even though their campground wasn't exactly what you would call quiet, the other bikers were respectful of each other's space. They lit a fire and relaxed with their group, making a few S'mores to ease themselves into food comas to help them sleep their road aches away.

In the morning Gene and Ellen hopped on their bike and headed to Rapid City. They ate breakfast at the Millstone Family Restaurant, loading up on omelets and pancakes. When they finished, they headed to Mount Rushmore National Monument. The walk up the path surrounded by flags from every state is always an experience, and the museum rotates exhibits so there is always something new to see. After hiking the monument trails they ate at the Exhibit Café before heading back. After several miles of roads twisting through pine forests in Badlands National Park they ended up back in Sturgis with the masses of metal monsters snorting through their exhausts.

The closest place to eat from where they parked was The Knuckle Brewing Company, known more for their micro brews than the pizzas and burgers they served. While they waited for their food, they talked about the most recent changes at Mount Rushmore. Every year there was a rumor they were opening the path to Gutzom Borglum's office and partially finished Hall of Records, but it always turned out to be a hoax. Maybe next year, they hoped.

"If we're even here next year," thought Gene to himself.

When their burgers arrived, they started talking about what they would do the rest of the week. Their aging bodies would appreciate a couple days off the bike. There were forest trails they could hike near their campsite to stretch their muscles and take pictures of birds. Nobody can duplicate the taste of burgers grilled in the smoke of a pine campfire, so that was something to look forward to. Evenings would be spent partying in town, so there would be no shortage of entertainment.

The other side trip Gene and Ellen always took during the

rally was to Deadwood. Although Gene enjoyed the scenery and history of Mount Rushmore, he looked forward to Deadwood the most. Growing up he learned he had a knack for gambling. During his time in the Army he earned enough playing cards to enjoy the best the locals had to offer when he had a weekend pass. It also allowed him to build a nest egg he used to buy a house when he came back from Vietnam and helped ease him through the time nobody would hire him because he was a soldier in an unpopular war.

Over the years his gambling hobby had turned into more of an obsession. He had monthly poker nights with his buddies, which his wife knew about and frequently helped host. After a while the low limits and predictable habits of his buddies lost his interest, though. He still attended the games and usually came out ahead, but the fascination with them cooled. Even their occasional trips to the Miami Valley and Hollywood Casinos seemed to just whet his appetite anymore, instead of satisfying his itch.

What he hadn't told Ellen was this trip to Sturgis was almost cancelled. He had started to bet on football, which he wasn't very good at, and had spent the money they saved for the trip on a "sure thing" a couple weeks before they were supposed to leave. If it hadn't been for a very successful night in a high stakes game just before they left, the trip would have been impossible-and they would have been a month behind on their mortgage, as well. Instead of satisfying his urge to gamble, the big win just fueled his desire to bet the house in Deadwood.

Ellen was somewhat uneasy about the trip to Deadwood this year. She enjoyed the beauty and history of the town, but there was something nagging at her. Gene had always been a good provider and a generous person, but he had changed the last couple of years. There were promises of gifts that didn't materialize, vacations that fell through "because of work" and less money going toward the causes they supported-even though he was making more money at work than ever. He had planned for retirement, but he started pushing back the date. There was something that she couldn't put her finger on that had her worrying about their finances in ways she hadn't thought about in years.

They took their nightly walk through the festivities after they left the restaurant. They turned left, exploring the opposite side of town. There were different vendors pitching their wares, along with a slightly different mix of food trucks to choose from. After checking out a few accessory booths, they split a funnel cake on the way back to their bike.

As they walked past one booth, someone handed him a card. He glanced at it briefly, wondering what they were selling since he didn't see any racks or food. It was an invitation to something called "Blessing of the Bikes" the next afternoon at the high school parking lot. He had heard about it before, but never attended. At this point he was desperate, and it might be a way to make sure they would at least have a way to get home after hitting the casinos in Deadwood, so why not?

It was relatively quiet the next morning, so they stayed at their campsite and played cards. The fire felt good against the morning chill, and the warmth fading from it signaled it was almost noon. Ellen heated up some chili in the kettle over the fire as Gene roasted bratwurst on the other side. The pine smoke gave the chili dogs an extra spark. They boiled some water from the stream and washed the dishes when they were done. With everything secured from the wildlife they headed out to see what this bike blessing was all about.

When they arrived at Sturgis Brown High School, the parking lot was about half full. There was a flatbed trailer on one end with a podium and sound system and people gathering around it, so they headed that direction. A lady with a CMA jacket greeted them and gave them bottles of water and pointed out a spot closer to the front they could park their bike.

Someone got up and introduced themselves. He said he was part of the Christian Motorcycles Association and described what they did. They set up booths at rallies like Sturgis to provide water and spiritual assistance, which was the most visible. They were also involved in local communities through poker runs and other volunteer efforts, as well as showing up to make noise in parades. The Blessing of the Bikes was where they would pray over each bike and its riders for protection for the coming year, and they would get a sticker to put on their bike.

As he was talking, Gene remembered getting drinks and something to snack on at a couple rest areas on the way that were run by CMA chapters. He was more interested in having one less meal to buy so he could gamble more than who put it on, but he did remember the patch they wore.

When the introduction was over, the MC introduced the main speaker. He called him Jesus, and he seemed to be popular with the volunteers there. There wasn't anything outstanding about him, and his leather jacket had seen better years. There were twelve others who got on stage with him, and they sang a few songs... enthusiastically, would be the best word for it. A small band backed them, which made the music tolerable at least.

When the music was over, Jesus started his talk. What he lacked in looks and style was quickly forgotten because of the sincerity and simple truth of his message. He talked about the thrill and freedom of the open road on a motorcycle that you can't find riding anything else. The theme changed to how you can experience the same freedom in your daily life by following God's plan for your life.

When the message ended, the MC closed with prayer and gave instructions on how to get your bike blessed. Those who chose to get the blessing walked their bikes in front of the stage, and there were several teams who performed the blessing. The ritual didn't last long, but those who experienced it seemed to walk a little lighter as they left.

Ellen shifted nervously while they waited, somewhat surprised Gene came to something like this in the first place and amazed he decided to have his bike blessed. She noticed he was deep in thought after the message and couldn't wait to find out what had gotten to him. She didn't have long to wait, though.

While most of the prayer teams worked their way down the line, the one Jesus led skipped around. After hitting a couple bikes in the front, he headed to them. He asked them where they were from and a few questions about their bike, then got to the point.

"Have you had your bike blessed before" Jesus asked?

"No, not really a religious person" Gene replied.

"So what brought you here today" Jesus queried?

"Oh, just getting old I guess, and we're a long way from home" Gene answered.

"That, and traffic seemed to be heavier this year," Ellen added.

"I see" Jesus said. "Is there anything else we can pray for while we're here?"

Any other time Gene would have brushed off the question. Actually, any other time he would have been sitting in a bar hoping the music and scenery would distract him from his troubles. That, and there was something about the man standing in front of him that was so sincere and easy to trust he couldn't help but open to him. He would do almost anything to have the mental freedom that he felt physically when he opened up the throttle of his bike.

Gene began telling Jesus about his gambling problem. Ellen's jaw dropped as he admitted how serious his problem was, and how it was affecting his family and the rest of his life. He admitted his desire to risk everything on the table was consuming the joy he used to get from his friends, family and having successes at his job.

Jesus asked a question now and then. While not intrusive, they were the right keys to opening what was on Gene's heart. The shadows on his face and shoulders lighted as he talked. Just being able to let someone else know what he was going through was a relief at this point. The tears in his eyes were mirrored in Ellen's as she was finally able to understand what had been haunting him for the last couple years.

When his story was done, Jesus told him how God could

replace the drive for more money with a peace and willingness to share with others once again. He suggested a couple groups who would hold him accountable through his journey, including a CMA chapter not far from where he lived.

Jesus put an arm around the shoulders of Gene and Ellen and prayed for him. The prayer was for Gene, but he also mentioned Ellen, their children and his work. As he prayed, Gene felt a warmth flow into him which filled his emptiness and soothed his aches.

After praying for them, Jesus and the rest of the team placed their gloved hands on their bike and prayed for their trips the rest of the year. Good roads, nice weather, mechanical soundness and pleasant companions. It was a classic Irish blessing decked out in chrome with glasspack mufflers.

When they finished, there were only a handful of bikes left in the parking lot. Gene and Ellen thanked them, then headed back to town for some food. They had a lot to talk about that night, and it would affect their future together in a positive way. The one thing they did know was this trip to Deadwood would be a different experience than any time they had gone there before.

Reflections

Proverbs 21:5 The plans of the diligent lead to profit as surely as haste leads to poverty.

At first you may have thought this story was about outlaw bikers, but they are hard to find. The typical biker now is your next-door neighbor. I don't think I have ever met an outlaw biker, but I know at least six preachers who ride bikes and use them to minister to other bikers on the road.

Gambling has also transitioned from something done behind closed doors in select locations to casinos scattered around the country and available to anyone over the internet. Lottery tickets are available in many gas stations, grocery stores and bars with only age restrictions. A bill was introduced in West Virginia to allow people to buy lottery tickets with credit or debit cards, enabling people to go deeper in debt trying to strike it big.

Gambling addiction is associated most with people who go to casinos and risk their money on several types of games, such as poker and sports. A gambling addiction is driven by three major factors. The first one is materialism, or the desire to have more. The second factor is getting a thrill from risking what you have for the chance to get a lot more. The last factor is using gambling as an escape from everyday life.

Questions for Contemplation

1. Based on the risk factors listed here, do you know anyone (including yourself) with a gambling addiction?

2. What resources are available in your area to treat someone with a gambling addiction?

3. A gambling addiction has many of the same symptoms and characteristics as drug addictions. While gambling doesn't have the same risk of death as taking drugs, the effects on an addict's family are similar. What kind of support can you provide the family of a gambling addict?

4. Since gambling devastates the finances of families, it can lead them to seek help with bills and food. Are you aware of any families seem to be economically stable but have started seeking help with basic needs that may fall into this category?

5. Gambling is one of the many issues most churches choose to avoid. It is hardly ever mentioned from the pulpit or discussed in Bible study groups. It is difficult to find a group for treating gambling problems that meet in a church. Why do you think gambling problems have become ignored by religious communities when they focus on so many other issues?

Call to Action

As with any issue, it is important to support those who are experiencing gambling addiction issues. Part of that is being willing to hear them tell their story and walking beside them to find help. This may include helping them with food and utilities when they have big losses. This can be draining on a personal level, so connecting with food banks and ministries who provide financial assistance would be important.

The national hotline for gambling addiction is run by Health and Human Services and is 1-800-662-HELP. Christian Drug Rehab is an organization who also treats gambling addiction. New Life Spirit Recovery is located in California, but it has several resources listed on its website. Christians in Recovery is another ministry that addresses gambling addictions. Your church should have contact information for local treatment resources as well.

19. THE TRANSITION

South Coast Hospice. The name has a pleasant ring to it, invoking images of a view of the beach on the Gulf of Mexico where one could spend their remaining days soaking up the sun as they listen to the waves washing ashore. Nice thought, except it sits in Coos Bay, Oregon, halfway between the Pacific Ocean and where Coos Bay hooks inland. Unfortunately, there are enough houses and businesses on either side you can't see either body of water from the hospice windows. If you are fortunate enough to have family close by, you might be able to convince them to take the short drive east or west to enjoy the view-if the biting cold of winter or smothering fog allows.

The facility itself is clean and maintained well. The staff are as pleasant and efficient as they can be, considering the environment they work in. Having a steady stream of rehab patients who recover takes some of the bite out of steadily losing the hospice patients who come their way. The rehab services help lower costs, as does their award-winning thrift store which frequently gets replenished when a hospice patient is lost.

Oliver Goodfellow was lucky, though. He had retired from logging two years ago but continued to supplement his retirement income by cutting firewood from slash piles left after trees were harvested. When he wasn't cutting wood, he would frequently go down to the bay and bring home as many fish as he could to smoke for the winter. Both of those activities came to a screeching halt when he slipped on a rock and broke his leg one afternoon, which led to the doctors discovering he had stage four pancreatic cancer. Even though they set his leg and began the rehab process, they predicted he would pass before he would be well enough to go back home.

While he was in the hospital, he got to know a group of former businessmen who visited the patients during the week. They were an assorted lot: several were fisherman, but they also included a carpenter and even an IRS agent. They had quit their jobs to go around the country teaching people how to be Christians. He never figured out why they ended up in Coos Bay, but from the stories he heard they were changing the lives of those that most religious people avoided and getting the religious people all riled up in the process.

After a couple of weeks in the rehab unit at the hospital, test results confirmed the doctor's suspicions. The bones were slowly knitting, but the cancer cells were multiplying faster. The cancer had mutated so the chemo wasn't effective any longer. After weighing the possibilities, Oliver decided to stop fighting the inevitable. He would end the treatments, which weren't working anyway, and spend his remaining days in South Coast Hospice just down the road from the hospital.

When it was time to make the move, the businessmen volunteered to help. They knew the executive director at South Coast and convinced her to let them borrow one of their vans for the event. Jesus, Philip and Andrew arrived just before lunch with a few empty boxes. It didn't take long for them to pack his belongings, and they were off.

Somewhere along the way they got lost. Instead of pulling up in front of the hospice, they ended up at his favorite lunch spot called Friend's Café. They loaded Oliver into his wheelchair and went in for lunch. Instead of eating the bland nutritious meals he had been suffering through while in the hospital, he plowed through a plate of fried shrimp and mashed potatoes with extra gravy. His nutritionist would have probably fainted, but he was with his friends here. His appetite had been sparse lately, but between his favorite food and being around friends he managed to eat it all and top it off with a bowl of their famous clam chowder and a salted caramel brownie sundae.

The familiar food helped Oliver gain enough courage to face his new environment. He got in the van and fell deep in thought about his life before cancer. When he came to himself again, he realized they were on another detour. Jesus was driving down the road by the coast where he had spent hours fishing and hunting. They drove a few miles out of town to the South Slough National Estuarine Research Reserve and stopped in the main parking lot.

They got out of the van and headed down the Middle Creek Trail. Going through the Douglas fir trees to the salt grass and sedge by the marshes brought back the tang of sea air diluted by the fumes around the hospital. The reminder of freedom was enhanced by a bald eagle circling overhead. A pair of herons floated just off the shore, feeding on the algae below. Even though his body was imprisoned by the wheelchair and cancer raging inside, his mind and soul were freed temporarily from the sterile walls which had constrained him the last few weeks.

When the late fall light began to fade, they piled back into the van and headed-for sure this time-to the hospice. When they arrived, they took him into his new room. The boxes were quickly unpacked and his possessions arranged under his direction. His last adventure for the day was meeting his new roommates in the dining room-at least the ones that could still leave their rooms to eat.

Time dragged in the hospice. Jesus and his friends visited Oliver and the other guests when they could, but there were few other visitors to distract from the waiting. He began reading the Bible the group left him to while away the hours and he watched hours of hunting and fishing shows on the TV to pass the time.

The cancer steadily progressed until Oliver could no longer get out of bed. It was hard for the logger and outdoorsman to depend on someone else to take care of his routine needs, but he didn't have a choice. He would tell them stories of the crazy things he had done and seen to distract from his reality. His strength and capabilities faded quickly, until only a shadow of his body and personality remained.

One day the entire group of businessmen showed up,

which was quite unusual. Jesus was even wearing a suit. This caused quite a stir, because this only happened when something big was going on and nobody had heard any rumors of anything unusual happening. After chatting for a few minutes with the staff, Jesus headed to Oliver's room with Mark and James while the rest wandered off to other rooms.

Oliver was breathing heavily when they got to his room. Pain was etched on his face behind the brave stoicism he maintained. His eyes were half-closed when they entered the room, and it took him a few minutes to recognize he had company. When he saw who it was, the spark in his eye brightened a bit.

"Must have been a meeting with a big donor for you to be in that git-up," Oliver said. "How much did you talk them into giving you?"

"Oh, they gave me everything they had." Jesus answered. "Most people wouldn't think it was much, but to them it was everything."

"I'd settle for a few hours in my cabin right now," Oliver rasped out as he struggled to breathe.

"You can have a cabin if you want it, but I'm afraid it will be made out of something other than the pine you love so much," Jesus answered.

"I'd settle for railroad ties if it would get me out of this room for a bit," Oliver whispered.

Jesus smiled down at him and took his hand. "Oh, I was thinking of something a little shinier than that."

Jesus motioned for Mark and James to come stand closer to the bed. He bent over the fragile frame in the bed and put one hand on his forehead for a bit. Oliver's face lightened into a smile, and the pain faded from his eyes.

"It is time for you to go home, my friend," Jesus said. "You have struggled through your course and won the prize."

The wall of the hospice faded, and a light began shining through it. Music played in the background, pure harmony reflecting the depths of nature with overtones of the cosmos. A burly figure in golden armor materialized beside Jesus.

"Oliver, you have reached the end of your journey," Jesus said. "You have followed the path set before you well and have done what I have asked you to do. Today you leave your mortal body and its cancer behind. You're going to have to hang out with the angels for a while, but I promise you will soon have a golden cabin out in the woods by a stream full of trout and salmon to keep you occupied."

With that, Oliver let out his last breath. Jesus held his hand and lifted his spirit out of his body. The angel standing beside them took his other hand, and they turned and left the room through the wall. The wall flashed back solid, and only his corpse remained in the room with the three men.

"Time to move on, men. Our job here is done," Jesus said.

With that they left the room. They motioned to the other men as they passed the rooms where they were, letting them know his fight was over. As they walked by the front door, they let the nurse on duty know there was one less patient they had to take care of.

As they left the hospice that afternoon it was cold and damp. The few leaves remaining on the trees outside rustled restlessly in the wind but seemed to have an extra glow shining through them. The sunlight was a little brighter perhaps than usual, and the breeze carried a hint of the music heard inside the room as Oliver was leaving.

Reflections

1 Corinthians 15:55 "Where, O death, is your victory? Where, O death, is your sting?"

They say the only things that are inevitable are death and taxes. It is the hope of most people to die quietly in their sleep after a long and healthy life. Unfortunately for many, death comes after a lengthy fight with diseases that rob them of their quality of life. For the unfortunate ones, hospice is a common way of allowing them to die in the best possible environment.

The key to death is being prepared. For Christians it is a transition to whatever you have experienced in this life to a better place without pain or disease. For those without Christ it is a scary leap into the unknown, which they hope ends with their last breath. For those who have put their faith in Christ, the knowledge of their future keeps them positive, even if they experience pain and suffering as they approach their last hours on Earth. Those without a hope in Christ can approach death without any pain and be surrounded by friends and family, but the fear of the unknown leads to torment in the end.

Questions for Contemplation

1. If you could choose where you will die, where would it be? Why would it be there?

2. If you knew you were going to die from a devastating disease, what changes would you make now to prepare for the experience?

3. How would knowing when you would die affect your life?

4. Having a disease like cancer or a stroke can be physically debilitating, and the treatment end up costing hundreds of thousands of dollars. Some people will keep demanding the newest drug and latest treatment

to extend their life, even if it is only for a matter of months. Have you ever considered the point where a longer life would not be worth the physical and financial cost of extending it? What would that point be?

5. It is hard to watch someone you know fade at the end of their life. Many deal with it by avoiding them, but this is not healthy for either the patient or the person who avoids them. What are the consequences of not supporting someone in their last stage of life, from not only a mental health perspective, but also how it affects their relationship with the rest of their family or friends? What are the spiritual consequences of not caring for those who are sick or dying?

Call to Action

The most important part of dealing with death is to know you are prepared for it. The only way to do this is to accept Christ as your personal savior, and to follow His instructions that are found in the Bible. Being prepared to step across the threshold of death, no matter when or how it comes, takes the fear out of the unknown. Those around you also benefit from your preparation because your life will follow God's instructions and you will care for not only your friends and family, but those in need in your community.

It is important to make sure those who are nearing the end know they are important and are cared for. This means you need to take the hard trips to see those who are only shadows of who they used to be. Including children in these trips is also important, so they begin to understand how temporary life is and how to care for those who are sick. It is also healthy to visit those in extended care facilities and hospices to share your caring with those who do not have visitors of their own.

There are many local programs and ministries to organize volunteers to visit with hospice patients. Many hospices are Christian ministries themselves and will train volunteers how to interact with their patients. "No One Dies Alone" is one program organized through the West Virginia University Healthcare program. Hospice Foundation of America and Xenos Christian Fellowship are two other organizations you can contact for more information about volunteering at hospices.

20. CONCLUSION

Matthew 25:40 "The King will reply, 'Truly I tell you, whatever you did for one of the least of these brothers and sisters of mine, you did for me.'

This book was born in a writers club at The Well Church in Manhattan, Kansas under the leadership of Gabe White. Although the club only lasted a couple years, it did get me back into the habit of writing and the theme of Jesus showing up in modern-day USA kept popping up when I was struggling with something to write for the month.

I'm sure there are some who would dismiss this book because of the basic premise. Jesus lived over two centuries ago, and the next time he comes to earth he will take charge instead of wandering around teaching like he did the first time. That part is true. However, until he comes Christians are instructed to be his hands and feet, fulfilling the mission of loving and caring for others. There are some who teach miracles can't happen today because they disappeared with the first century church, but Jesus taught we would be able to do what he did after he left.

The key to being the hands and feet of Christ lies in accepting the presence of Holy Spirit. Humans are truly incapable of performing miracles, even though doctors sometimes come close. It is not what we can do, but what we allow Holy Spirit to do through us. The modern-day miracles I have seen tend to come through what is considered the Pentecostal movement. Most fundamental Christians are told they must accept and give control to Holy Spirit, but only as long as He fits into the box where it doesn't lead to such crazy things as speaking in tongues and dancing and performing miracles. It is little wonder we see

so few miracles in our time.

As I was writing the chapter on Giving for "The Financial Cornerstone," I had the same thoughts I'm sure many would have when reading it. If money given through the church fell under either the tithes or offerings categories, I didn't really know any local ministries to give gifts to. That is when I realized I had a way of addressing it, which covered a broad range of those in need to help stretch our visions.

I realized as I was writing that it is not so much about opening eyes to those in need around us, but also about our understanding of what ministry should be focused on and how far many modern churches have strayed from that vision. That is why each chapter not only has a Call to Action where you can help those who are affected by the topic, but also questions about how you think about, and act towards, that group of people as well.

It also becomes obvious people tend to fit in more categories than one. For example, my first financial client grew up in Coos Bay, Oregon where the hospice story is based. As he grew up he got into riding motorcycles and was a member of the Christian Motorcycle Association for many years, including the chapter I served as treasurer in for awhile. As an adult he became a preacher, then ended his career at a truck driver. I spent a night with him as a lumper in his truck at the truck stop in Denver where the human trafficking story is based. While I did not intend to include fragments of his life in so many of these stories, he showed up in them anyway.

If I included a story for every group of people who are mission fields within a few miles of every one of us, it would take several more months to finish. Here are a few more questions to help grow your vision and potential giving options after this book goes on your shelf.

Questions for Contemplation

1. Did you personally identify with any of the situations in this book?

2. Were there any situations in this book that made you uncomfortable? Why or why not?

3. Are there other situations you are aware of where you and your local church are or could have a positive influence in? One example I considered is illegal aliens.

4. If you had unlimited resources, what group would you focus your time and finances to help?

5. What is preventing you from making a difference in that situation right now?

6. If someone had unlimited resources to help a situation you are in yourself, what would the most effective ways they could they address it?

7. The most common reason people don't get involved with making a positive difference in someone else's life is they are too busy. List the things that take up the most of your time and consider if they fit into a life devoted to serving others.

8. List the largest needs you know of in your community.

9. List the programs your church supports and match them to the community needs you just listed.

10. Are there programs your church could offer that would better care for your community, or would they be served better outside a church environment?

ABOUT THE AUTHOR

Philip Brown

Philip Brown is a poet, story teller, financial educator, scientist and gardener mixing a few elements of each into his writings. He uses examples from everyday life to explain more complex principles, showing a different perspective on what many try to make complicated. He considers his garden to be a metaphor for life: large, full of a wide variety of plants, and meant to be shared to its fullest.

BOOKS BY THIS AUTHOR

The Financial Cornerstone

Are you tired of books telling you how to manage money without giving you any background?

Fed up with inspirational money management seminars that focus on financial techniques but seem to forget about the Biblical basis they claim to teach? Ever wonder why following all the popular money management techniques still seems to result in the same circumstances you started in?

Budgets and techniques are useful tools, but if your heart is not right with God and your spiritual relationship is built on the wrong fundamentals then finances are an easy target. By putting God first in your finances, you can free yourself from the lure of materialism and misaligned priorities, allowing you to be blessed financially and achieve God's planned prosperity for your life.

www.ingramcontent.com/pod-product-compliance
Lightning Source LLC
Chambersburg PA
CBHW032005170626
46807CB00006B/2655